"I'm going to see to it that you and Zach get together," Kit told Jessica firmly over the phone.

"How are you going to do that?" Jessica asked, an edge of uncertainty in her voice. "I don't even know for sure if he likes me."

"Zach likes you, all right," Kit assured her. "He's just shy, that's all." She felt a sudden pressure in her throat, but she took a deep breath.

"You really are a great friend!" Jessica said enthusiastically.

"Yeah, that's me," Kit replied, trying to sound cheerful. "Always a bridesmaid, never a bride."

There was a startled silence on the other end of the phone. "What do you mean by that?" Jessica asked finally.

"It means that you and Zach will be getting together," Kit said brightly. "And I'll be right there, cheering you guys on."

After she hung up the phone, Kit slumped against the kitchen cabinet. Now she, Kit Carson, was the official matchmaker for Jessica Finch and Zachary Taylor.

Bantam Sweet Dreams Romances
Ask your bookseller for the books you have missed

Practice Makes Perfect

Jahnna Beecham

BANTAM BOOKS
TORONTO • NEW YORK • LONDON • SYDNEY • AUCKLAND

RL 6, IL age 11 and up

PRACTICE MAKES PERFECT
A Bantam Book / July 1988

ISBN 0-553-27276-4

Published simultaneously in the United States and Canada

*Bantam Books are published by Bantam Books, a division of Bantam
Doubleday Dell Publishing Group, Inc. Its trademark, consisting of the
words "Bantam Books" and the portrayal of a rooster, is Registered in
U.S. Patent and Trademark Office and in other countries. Marca
Registrada. Bantam Books, 666 Fifth Avenue, New York, New York 10103.*

PRINTED IN THE UNITED STATES OF AMERICA

O   0 9 8 7 6 5 4 3 2 1

*For our dear friends
Kathy, Bob, and Baby Peter.*

Chapter One

"Tony Roman, if you ever give me an assignment like this again, I'll strangle you!"

Kit Carson tore a sheet of paper from her typewriter and threw it at the feet of the editor in chief. Then she pulled her black felt hat down over her eyes and announced, "I give up!"

Melanie Billings, a junior working on the pasteup of the advertising section, grumbled, "Darn! This picture is crooked!"

Tony ran a hand through his thick dark hair and grinned. "Ah, yes! Business as usual here at the *Queen Anne High Spectator*—Seattle's finest high-school newspaper!"

Kit slipped another page into the old Underwood typewriter and started pounding furiously on the keys. She held a yellow pencil between her teeth, and every few minutes she let out a yowl of frustration.

"Hang in there, Kit," Tony said, patting his star reporter on the shoulder.

Two typewriter keys jammed, and Kit looked up at her friend in disgust.

"Why don't you give this a break," Tony suggested, "and help me with the photo spread?"

"Gladly!" Kit hopped up from her chair and followed him to the long center table that held the *Spectator* layout. Tony pointed to the three photos that dominated the front page.

"Well, what do you think?"

Kit picked up one of the pictures and looked at it closely. "Hey, this is me!" she exclaimed.

"You're very observant," Tony said.

Kit jabbed him with her elbow and studied the photo critically. It was one of her on the job, covering the latest pep rally. Kit examined her outfit—baggy pleated pants, bright red suspenders, and one of her signature hats —a red beret.

"I think I need another haircut," Kit said, putting the picture back on the table. She smoothed her short brown hair and brushed her long bangs out of her eyes.

"I'm not talking about the picture," Tony said. "What do you think of the caption?"

Kit chewed her pencil thoughtfully while Tony read aloud: " 'Queen Anne High's ace reporter, Kit Carson, keeps an eagle eye out for her latest scoop.' "

"I like the 'ace reporter' bit." Kit raised one eyebrow at her friend. "But you left out the most important part."

"Oh?" Tony scratched his head and reached for a note pad. "What's that?"

Kit put her hand behind her head and struck an exaggerated model's pose. "I am also considered a famous beauty, fashion trendsetter, and heartthrob of millions!"

Tony snorted loudly and tossed the note pad back onto the desk.

"You can't blame me for trying!" Kit shrugged. She certainly wouldn't describe herself as beautiful. Interesting was a better word. Her clear brown eyes sparkled above strong cheekbones that, Kit was relieved to see, had emerged from beneath the baby fat that tormented her in junior high.

Tony nudged Kit with his elbow, snapping her out of her reverie. "What do you think of this?" he asked, flipping another photograph in front of her. It showed a pensive Tony, hands in his pockets, strolling along the Seattle waterfront.

"Not bad," Kit said. "You look almost human."

"Thank you," Tony replied politely. Then he crossed his eyes and did a slathering wolf impersonation that set Kit giggling.

Tony had been her pal for almost three years now, ever since ninth grade. That was when they'd both shown up in journalism class the first day of school. Now they were juniors, both working on the *Spectator*, and Tony had risen all the way to editor.

Kit preferred to cover the school-activities beat. She was best known for her weekly column, "Kit's Korner." Her free-ranging, slightly off-center observations on life and love had won her the reputation of being the best writer at Queen Anne High.

"So whose idea was it, anyway, to do a feature story on us?" Tony demanded.

"Melanie's, I think." Kit gestured toward the pretty blonde standing across from her. "You know how Mel *loves* to have her picture taken!" she added wickedly.

"That's not fair," Melanie retorted, tossing an eraser at Kit. "It was Mr. Cunningham's idea. He said it was high time that Queen Anne students got to know their own newspaper staff."

At the mention of his name, the group's faculty advisor glanced up from his cluttered desk in the corner and smiled vaguely in their direction. The absent look on his face usually meant he was deep in thought. He had a small mustache and wore a funny bow tie. Kit thought he was a bit peculiar at times, but she, along with everyone else in the school, adored Mr. Cunningham.

"Speaking of staff," Tony said, "have you noticed that there are only five of us in here once again?"

"Mmm," Kit agreed, glancing quickly around the room. Aside from herself, Tony, and Melanie, the only others working on the paper were Brian Thompson and Sam Pond. They sat huddled in front of a computer monitor, busily entering formatting data onto the terminal.

"You know," Tony continued, shaking his head, "I still can't get over Bob Hamma quitting on us like that. He was our entire sports department."

"He couldn't take the long hours," Melanie said. "His grades were starting to suffer."

"Yeah, but how did I end up with his job?" Kit asked, pointing to her typewriter. "Here I am, writing a feature article on basketball, which happens to be one sport I know nothing about."

"What?" Tony said, collapsing against his desk in a mock faint. "The great Kit Carson admits to not knowing something?"

"You're asking for it, Tony," Kit replied evenly, pushing up the sleeves of her white work coat. She had worn the coat as a uniform in the *Spectator* office for two years, and it was covered with ink spots.

"We really need some new blood," Melanie said. "Maybe we should print a Help Wanted sign along with this article."

"That would defeat the purpose of the issue," Tony observed wryly. "This edition is supposed to show that we are doing just fine and that the *Spectator* richly deserves its high ranking in state competition."

"But what about all those guys?" Kit pointed to the staff portrait on the wall. It had been taken during the second week of school. Kneeling in the front row were Tony, Melanie, Kit, Brian, and Sam. Behind them, smiling at the camera, stood four handsome senior guys in letter jackets, with three pretty girls between them.

"Seriously, folks," Kit went on, "why is it that we do all the work . . ."

"And *they* share the credit!" Melanie and Tony finished for her.

"What's all this grumbling I hear?" Mr. Cunningham called from his desk. "Dissension in the ranks?"

Kit jerked her thumb toward the picture.

"We couldn't help noticing that, once again, as another tight deadline approaches, our golden boys and girls have left us in the lurch."

"Mr. C, we need some help!" Tony pleaded.

"I'm glad you brought that up." Mr. Cunningham adjusted his bow tie and pushed his chair back from the desk. "I'm supposed to meet with a new recruit this afternoon." He glanced down at his watch. "As a matter of fact, he should be here any minute."

"Yeah?" Tony's ears perked up, but just as quickly his shoulders sagged. "Who are we kidding? He'll probably be like the others."

"Right," Kit chimed in. "Joining the newspaper staff to pad his college applications."

"I believe you're all becoming a bit too cynical," Mr. Cunningham chastened gently.

"Can he type?" Melanie demanded.

"And has he ever worked on a paper before?" Kit asked, knowing all too well the likely answer.

"Yes to both questions," a voice replied from the doorway.

Kit could feel the warmth rushing to her cheeks as she spun around to see who had spoken. Out of the corner of her eye she noticed that Melanie looked a little embarrassed, too.

"I was assistant editor for the *Columbia*

High Monitor in Portland, Oregon." The tall, lean figure was silhouetted in the doorway. "I'm pretty handy with a word processor, and anything I don't know I can learn."

The newcomer stepped into the room, and Kit was finally able to get a good look at him. What struck her first was the way he walked, in easy, swinging movements. His smile was slightly crooked, warm, and friendly. It seemed to go naturally with his sandy blond hair and twinkling blue eyes.

"I'm Zachary Taylor," he said introducing himself. "And, please," he added quickly, "no president jokes—I've heard them all!"

He stuck out his hand to Kit, and she shook it briskly. "Kit Carson," she said with a grin. "And if you make any explorer jokes, I'll bean you!"

"Hey!" Tony said, snapping his fingers. "Didn't Kit Carson and Zachary Taylor live around the same time?"

"Yes, I believe they did." Mr. Cunningham nodded and straightened his tie. "Kit Carson was an army scout, and Taylor was a general in the war against Mexico. They probably even worked together."

"Looks like you two were made for each other." Tony snickered.

"It *is* pretty amazing," Zach said, directing his crooked grin right at Kit.

She felt a sudden, odd pressure in her chest, but she met his gaze steadily. "Our parents must have studied child naming at the same school of torture," she said.

"Right!" Zach replied with a chuckle.

"Now, before the Inquisition here works you over," Mr. Cunningham interrupted, "I'd just like to say, welcome to our little zoo. Maybe I can explain exactly what it is we do around here."

"Sounds good to me." Zach leaned back on the edge of a nearby desk and listened intently as Mr. Cunningham began to talk. He looked right at home in the newsroom. He was wearing baggy twill pants and a worn tweed sport coat, with the sleeves pushed up.

Kit smiled. *Zachary Taylor,* she thought, *I like your style.*

"And what are you grinning at?" the ever-watchful Tony whispered in her ear.

"Our new recruit," Kit whispered back. "I think he'll fit in just fine."

"I hate to be a wet blanket, guys," Melanie announced, "but we have a deadline to meet and only one hour to do it in."

"An hour!" Kit and Tony blurted out at the same moment.

Instantly the room became a flurry of activity. Kit raced for her typewriter to finish her article. Tony hastily grabbed a ruler and started measuring the headline spacing. Even Mr. Cunningham was roused into action, joining Melanie on pasteup.

"Zach, give Kit a hand with that basketball feature," Tony ordered brusquely. "Remember, you've only got three column inches—so make it fit!"

Zach nodded and turned to Kit, his eyebrows raised slightly. "You're the sports writer?"

The edge of doubt in his voice made her temper flare. "Why? You think a girl can't write intelligently about basketball?"

"No, that's not what I meant at all!" Zach shook his head, then asked quickly, "Where's the copy?"

As she handed him her draft, Kit regretted her sharp words. Why hadn't she just admitted that sports were something she knew next to nothing about, and let it go? She was sure he would have understood. Now she was going to look like an idiot in front of a guy she hardly knew.

Zach glanced up from the page and regarded Kit curiously.

"What's the matter?" she blurted out.

"You're good." His voice was low and sounded very sincere. "Really good."

Kit felt her face grow beet-red in spite of herself. "Thanks," she murmured.

"The way you described a slam-dunk was great!" He looked down at her copy again and read aloud. "And like a thunderbolt, he falls!"

"That's from Tennyson's poem 'The Eagle,' " Kit confessed. "I've always loved that line."

"Well, it's fantastic!" He smiled and added, "Just like Red Smith."

Kit felt a warm glow suffuse her body. She knew Red Smith had been one of the greatest sportswriters who had ever lived.

"Now the bad news," Zach continued. "You've got your terms all mixed up. Why don't you axe this line and shift this phrase up into your lead? That'll tighten your opening paragraph and make it more dramatic." Zach scratched out lines as he spoke and made notes on the margins with a felt-tip pen. Finally he flipped his edited version of the article back to Kit. "So what do you think?"

Kit scanned the feature. A smile crept across her face, and she looked back at Zach. "You're not so bad, yourself."

"Have you got that piece ready to go yet?" Tony yelled. "Or are you two just going to stand around and mutually admire each other's work?"

This time they both blushed, and Kit hurriedly shoved the sheet into Tony's hand. "Here's the copy."

Tony looked it over and said, "Perfect. There's only one problem; the voice isn't really yours anymore, Kit. It's definitely more masculine."

"That's easy to fix," Kit replied, snatching the page from Tony's hands and adding Zach's name to the byline. "There. 'By Kit Carson and Zachary Taylor.' "

Tony grinned like a cat. "Okay, Woodward and Bernstein, let's get cracking. We've got a paper to get out!"

For the rest of the hour, Kit and Zach worked on two more articles. One was a feature Kit had done on Scholar-of-the-Month. Zach deleted a few flowery adjectives and tightened up a sentence or two.

Kit adjusted her glasses on her nose as she watched Zach type their changes into the article. She realized that she was already very comfortable working with him, as if they'd been friends forever. There didn't seem to be any awkwardness between them at all.

At exactly three minutes to five, Melanie called, "Time!"

Kit hastily gathered the pages she and Zach had been working on and handed them to Tony, who arranged them in the proper order. Then the editorial staff took a few minutes to survey their work and double-check it for errors. When they had finished Tony announced, "I'll drive this down to the printer's now. Want to ride with me, Kit?"

"Hey, Tony, I'd like to go along," Zach said from across the room. "Maybe on the way you can give me some pointers on writing for the *Spectator*."

"I'll go too," Melanie called. "We'll tell Zach all about Seattle."

"And if you join us, Kit," Tony said, scooping up the copy under his arm, "you can fill Zach in on all the school dirt."

"Dirt?" Zach asked, focusing his vibrant blue eyes on Kit.

"Tony is referring to my column, 'Kit's Korner,' " she explained primly. "It does have some gossip but I like to think it has a lot of substance, too."

"Let's put it this way," Melanie said. "If something's happening at Queen Anne High, Kit is the first to know about it. Everyone confides in her."

Kit was going to respond, but at that moment Jerry Gill, a short, muscular guy wearing a Queen Anne letter jacket, stuck his head in the door.

"Hey, Kit," Jerry said, apparently oblivious of the fact that she was standing there with her mouth half-open. "Have you got a minute?"

Kit's throat felt very dry, but she finally managed to stammer, "Uh, sure, Jerry."

"Then can I talk to you?" the handsome football player asked. "It's real important."

"Well, sure, Jerry!" Kit thought her voice sounded impossibly breathy and high-pitched. "I'll meet you in the commons in—five minutes, okay?"

"Great." Jerry disappeared around the corner, and Kit wanted to shout with happiness. The boy she had had a crush on for two whole months had finally spoken to her!

Kit reached up and touched her cheek. It was burning, and she knew her face was probably bright red. Spinning back to face her desk, she caught Zach looking at her oddly.

"That was Jerry Gill," Kit explained, giggling slightly. Zach was still staring at her, so she added, "Jerry's a senior. He's on the football team."

"He's also supposed to be on the staff of this paper," Tony cut in. "But, as you can see, he didn't feel it was necessary to show up today."

"Not everyone is as single-minded as you are, Tony," Kit replied, removing her lab coat and tossing it on its usual hook. "I mean, there *are* other important things in life besides paper and ink."

"Name two!" Tony snapped back.

Kit stuck her tongue out at him and continued, "Anyway, I have to talk to Jerry, so I guess I won't be able to go to the printer's with you."

Kit felt herself blushing again as she said Jerry's name, so she quickly turned her attention to shoving pens into her book bag.

"Remember, everybody," Mr. Cunningham announced to the *Spectator* staff, "tomorrow at two-thirty for the post-mortem."

There was a chorus of good-natured groans from the staff as they filed from the room. Mr. Cunningham flicked off the lights and locked the door behind them.

"Give Jerry our best!" Tony called to Kit, a little too sweetly.

"I sure will," Kit replied. She stood for a moment, watching the chattering group recede into the distance, before she turned and floated toward the commons.

I wonder what Jerry wants to talk to me about? Kit thought. A dreamy smile played across her lips as she mused about the possibilities. *A date? The school dance? No, probably something more casual, like getting together for a Coke. Maybe he wants me to help him with his English homework.*

Her footsteps slowed. *Maybe he wants the*

answers to the pop quiz in Moynihan's comp lit class. Kit shook her head. *No, he already got those from Mike Peters.* She bit her lip. *What else could it be?*

Suddenly her knees locked, and she gasped. The realization had come so clear and strong that it felt like a punch in the stomach.

Kit knew exactly what Jerry wanted to talk to her about. Why hadn't she thought of it immediately? It was the same thing every other guy in school wanted to talk with her about. *Jessica Finch.*

Chapter Two

"She hasn't spoken to me in three days." Jerry Gill slumped down on one of the marble benches in the commons and sighed heavily.

Jessica Finch was Kit's best friend. They met in kindergarten, shortly after Jessica had moved to Seattle from Wisconsin. Sweet and unselfish by nature, Jessica, the tiny blond girl with eyes as blue as cornflowers, had grown into the prettiest girl at Queen Anne High. Jessica attracted guys like bees to honey. *And now,* Kit thought morosely, *Jerry Gill had fallen under her spell.*

The handsome senior tugged at his dark, wavy hair in frustration. "So what'd I do wrong, anyway?"

Kit bit her lip hard. She wanted to shout,

"You picked the wrong girl! Jessica doesn't want you as a boyfriend—I do! I'm the one who has a crush on you, can't you see that?" Instead she forced herself to smile and say, "I'm sure you didn't do anything wrong. She's probably just preoccupied."

Her answer made Jerry slump even farther down on the bench.

"Jessica's been really busy lately," Kit assured him. "Her gymnastics training takes up most of her time, and she had that big test today in honors French."

"I know, I know," Jerry acknowledged reluctantly. He gazed up at her, and Kit felt lucky that at least he was talking to her. That in itself was a major breakthrough.

"Besides, Jessica is actually kind of shy," Kit continued, trying to position herself on the bench in what she hoped was an elegant pose.

"Really?" Jerry arched a dubious eyebrow in her direction, and Kit noticed a ragged little scar above it.

"Oh, she's a lot of fun when we're all just hanging around together," Kit explained, "but one-on-one with a guy—that's a different story."

"She's shy, huh?" Jerry absorbed this new information for a moment.

18

"So if Jess hasn't talked to you lately, I'm sure it wasn't deliberate."

"You mean she hasn't said anything bad about me?" Jerry asked, sounding hopeful.

Kit shook her head. "Not a word." She neglected to add that Jessica hadn't said anything about him at *all*. The only time Jerry Gill's name was mentioned in any of their conversations was when Kit herself brought it up. Which had been rather often, lately.

"I'm glad to hear that." The rugged senior sat up and stretched his arms out languorously. "So, if I ask Jessica out, she probably won't turn me down, right?"

Before Kit could stammer out a reply, Jerry said, "That's just what she needs. An outgoing guy like me to loosen her up a little." He winked at Kit and added cockily, "When it comes to one-on-one, it's hard to resist the old Gill charm."

Kit couldn't believe her ears. Gone was the vulnerable boy who needed consolation and advice, and in his place was a swaggering football star brimming with self-confidence.

"Hey, Kit, good deal," Jerry said, punching her lightly on the shoulder. "I'll see you around, okay?"

She watched him saunter away, out through big glass doors of the school. *Why does ev-*

ery guy who goes nuts for Jessica have to talk to me about it first? Kit wondered. *It would be nice if someone got a crush on me occasionally.*

Kit stood up and looped her book bag over her shoulder. *Maybe I'm just not the romantic type,* she thought miserably.

In her own way, Kit knew she was as popular as Jessica. The guys all confided in her because they trusted her.

And that's almost as good, she told herself as she stepped out into the gray Seattle afternoon. *Almost.*

At ten to twelve the next day, Kit was jolted awake by the school bell bringing third period and Mrs. Foster's European history class to an end. She sat up and quickly looked around to see if anyone had noticed her napping.

Although European history *did* get pretty boring at times, there was another reason Kit was feeling so tired that morning. She had spent a restless night thinking about Jerry Gill and all the other boys who had failed to notice her. She had finally fallen asleep by counting what she considered to be her numerous personality flaws.

A gnawing rumble in her stomach reminded Kit that it was lunchtime. She stuffed her notes into her book bag and quickly made her way to the door.

"So, where are you and Jess eating today?" Melanie asked as they shuffled down the tiled hallway toward the lunchroom.

"Outside, I hope," Kit replied, adjusting her bright red beret. "If the weather's nice enough."

"Well, if the past few weeks are any indication," Melanie said darkly, "you'll have drizzle, drizzle, and more drizzle."

Seattle certainly had its share of wet weather. Usually Kit didn't notice the rain, but it had been dragging on for three weeks now, and she was beginning to feel a little down.

"Yesterday the sun peeked out for a minute, then just disappeared." Kit sighed heavily. "Soon we'll all have webbed feet."

Entering the cafeteria, Kit paused and quickly scanned the bustling lunchroom. Groups of kids staked out certain tables and sat at them every day. The table by the door was always reserved for the student government types. The drama club naturally sat in the center of all the action. The jocks held court by the window, with the cheerleaders encamped nearby. The rest of the tables were for the undecided.

Kit preferred to table-hop because it gave her a chance to keep up with the latest news flying around Queen Anne High. Her columns were filled with little tidbits of recent conversation that she'd overheard in the lunchroom —funny comments, new jokes, or some worthy cause that needed mentioning. However, she and Jessica always managed to spend some time together during the lunch hour.

"Judging from the deep thicket of letter jackets over by the window," Melanie said, pointing, "my guess is that Jessica is seated right there."

"Listen, Melanie," Kit said, as her friend stepped into the lunch line, "I'll catch you later in journalism, okay?"

When Kit reached the table, the boys made room for her to sit down next to Jessica. Kit realized, not for the first time, how proud she was to be Jessica's best friend.

"Kit, I've been looking all over for you!" Jessica reached out and squeezed Kit's hand warmly. "I've got some wonderful news! I wanted you to be the first to know." Jessica's pretty blue eyes glittered with excitement. Turning back to her admirers she said lightly, "Listen, guys, I don't mean to be rude, but I'd like to talk to Kit for a bit, okay?"

A disappointed rumbling met her announcement. Jessica flashed a dazzling smile to any opposition, and the boys obediently got up and moved to another table. Kit shook her head in amazement.

"What's the matter?" Jessica asked, dipping a spoon into her yogurt carton.

"I just can't get over how you can turn these tough macho guys into grateful little puppy dogs with one tiny dose of that Finch charm."

Jessica laughed, her face turning a soft pink.

"Okay," Kit ordered, "tell me the big news."

Jessica opened her mouth to speak, but her smile suddenly faded. "Kit?" she said, leaning toward her friend. "Are you all right?"

The concern in Jessica's voice frightened Kit. "Why?" she asked. "Do I look funny?" She felt her face. "Do I have the measles or something?"

"No, no, nothing like that," Jessica said with a chuckle. "You seem a little tired, that's all."

Kit heaved a sigh of relief and then drooped with one elbow on the table. "That's because I *am* tired. I just snoozed through Foster's European history trying to make up for not getting any sleep last night."

"What happened last night?" Jessica dipped her spoon back into her strawberry yogurt.

"I just couldn't get to sleep," Kit mumbled. "I was too busy thinking."

"About what?"

"Like, why do I always fall for guys who don't know I'm alive? And why do I get punches on the shoulder from them instead of kisses on the lips?" Kit sighed. "You know, important stuff like that."

"Those are awful questions to ask yourself!" Jessica's forehead was wrinkled with concern.

"If you think the questions are bad, you should hear the answers." In a singsong tone, Kit started ticking her faults off on her fingers. "I'm fat, I'm ugly, I wear glasses—"

"And you exaggerate," Jessica interrupted. "Okay, so you were a little chubby in junior high, but that was a long time ago. What you are now is pretty, witty, and, best of all, completely original!" Jessica grinned. "You do, however, wear glasses."

"Ohh!" Kit groaned and covered her eyes.

Jessica set her yogurt cup down on the table and crossed her arms. "This wouldn't have anything to do with Jerry Gill by any chance, would it?"

Kit raised her eyebrows. "How did you know that?"

"I'm your best friend. You can't hide anything from me." With one hand, Jessica flipped her shiny blond hair over her shoulder. "Besides, Jerry is all you've talked about for the last month. He's first on your prospective date list, isn't he?"

"Well, you can scratch him off *my* list and move him over to yours."

"What does that mean?" Jessica asked, cocking her head.

"It means that Jerry Gill"—Kit made a sweeping gesture to the cafeteria—"like each and every one of the other handsome, available guys at Queen Anne, has fallen under the Jessica Finch spell."

"How do you know that?"

"He told me. And, like an idiot, I sat there and listened."

"Oh, Kit," Jessica began, "that's aw—"

"What it boils down to," Kit interrupted, "is that I still don't have a boyfriend."

"Well, if it makes you feel any better," Jessica said, putting her arm around Kit's shoulder, "I don't, either."

"Yeah, but that's your choice." Kit suddenly sat up straight. "How are you ever going to find true love if you keep turning guys away?" she demanded.

"Just because someone likes you doesn't mean that you're going to like him back." Jessica twisted one strand of her blond hair around her finger and went on. "Dates make

25

me so uncomfortable. I never know what to say when I'm alone with a boy." She shrugged. "I guess I don't want to go out with anyone unless I really care about him."

"And how are you ever going to know *that* unless you go out with him first?" Kit asked, exasperated.

"You've got a point," Jessica admitted.

Kit gestured grandly around them at the noisy lunchroom. "Somewhere out there are two perfect guys—"

"Just waiting for two perfect girls," Jessica finished for her. "Hey, wait a minute," she said suddenly. "I still haven't told you my good news!"

"So, tell me now!" Kit snapped to attention and waited expectantly.

Jessica took a deep breath, then blurted out, "Ms. Ericksen has chosen me to represent Queen Anne High in the state invitational gymnastics tournament!"

"Oh, Jess, that's fantastic!" Kit shouted, jumping up to hug her friend.

"Isn't it? I'm already nervous. The meet is less than a month away."

"Well, I'll be cheering the loudest when you win the gold," Kit replied.

"I wish you could come with me," Jessica said anxiously. "Maybe I wouldn't get so nervous."

"Hey, if I offered to cover the meet for the *Spectator*, they might let me go along. I could get a press pass and everything." Kit dug into her book bag for her note pad and began scribbling furiously. "We could do a whole series, following you from your humble beginnings here in Seattle all the way to the nationals. What do you think?"

"I think you're jumping the gun a little," Jessica replied with a giggle. "But I do appreciate your confidence in me." She reached over and squeezed Kit's hand.

Kit looked up and smiled proudly at her pal. "What are friends for?"

There was a loud burst of laughter from a tableful of boys in the far corner.

"Hey, there's Jerry Gill," Kit said, surprised she hadn't noticed him right away. She and Jessica watched as Jerry took his butter and tossed it in the air. There was another roar from his companions as the pat of butter stuck to the ceiling.

"What's so funny about that?" Kit asked, cocking one eyebrow.

"Nothing," Jessica answered, shaking her head. "But it's typical of Jerry's brand of humor."

Kit was surprised to hear the sharp tone of disapproval in her friend's voice. "Don't you like Jerry?"

"Not very much, no," Jessica confessed.

"Why didn't you—" Kit started to shout, but Jessica gestured for her to lower her voice. "Why didn't you tell me that?" Kit whispered.

"I didn't say anything before because you seemed so crazy about him." Jessica gave an apologetic half smile. "I'm sorry."

"I don't even know him, really," Kit remarked. She watched as Jerry crumpled his milk carton, aimed at one of the trash cans in the corner, tossed, and missed.

"I don't think you want to," Jessica drawled. A scowling lunchroom monitor strode toward the table of boys just as the bell rang.

"See you later," Jessica called as she scooped up her books. "Remember, somewhere out there are two perfect guys!"

Kit watched her friend race for the exit. "I won't hold my breath," she muttered to herself.

Chapter Three

Kit suddenly realized that she hadn't gotten anything to eat and hurried to the cafeteria line to buy an apple. Taking a loud, crunchy bite of the fruit, she headed for her creative writing class. Kit lifted the flap on her book bag as she walked and searched with one hand for the day's assignment.

"Let's see," she muttered between chomps, "I made breakfast, finished my French paper, and looked for Gramps' glasses. Then I grabbed my assignment off the kitchen counter and helped Gramps load the laundry into the washer."

Kit stopped in the middle of the hallway, recreating her actions in the right order. When she got as far as the laundry, Kit wailed, "Oh, no! I washed my writing assignment with the dirty clothes!" Pulling her hat down over her forehead, she collapsed against a nearby locker.

"That's one way to stamp out yellow journalism," a warm baritone sounded from beside her.

Kit peeked out from under her beret and found herself looking straight into Zachary Taylor's blue eyes.

" 'Yellow journalism'?" she repeated, raising one eyebrow.

"It was a small joke." He grinned crookedly, then added, "Okay—a tiny one."

"Pretty minuscule." Kit smiled back.

The tardy bell rang, and she sprang away from the locker. "Mrs. Hubbard isn't going to like my coming in empty-handed," she said, beginning to move down the hall toward the stairs. "Where are you headed?" she called back over her shoulder.

"I was about to ask you to help me decipher this schedule," Zach explained, trotting along beside her. He was clutching a piece of white paper. "But you were so busy mumbling to yourself, and making those bizarre gestures, that I thought it'd be safer to keep my distance till whatever came over you had run its course."

"That's my memory dance," Kit said with

an embarrassed laugh, leading Zach up the stairs. "It's the best way to figure out where I've misplaced something. My grandfather taught it to me. I reenact whatever I did, and it jogs my memory."

"Not a bad idea."

"It does have its drawbacks." Kit laughed. "Like making a fool of myself in public places."

"Fool, I think, is the wrong word," Zach said with a grin. "*Spectacle* is more like it."

"Kit Carson!" a voice boomed from the foot of the stairs. "What are you doing out of class?"

Kit nearly leapt out of her skin. The voice belonged to Mr. Purvis, the assistant principal. It was just her luck to have him catch her in the hall without a pass.

"I'm—uh—on my way to class now, and, um . . ." Her mind suddenly went blank.

"Kit is helping me find my next class," Zach offered quickly, coming to her rescue. "I'm new at Queen Anne. My name is Zachary Taylor."

"Zachary Taylor?" Mr. Purvis repeated, his voice full of disbelief.

"Yes, sir," Zach replied. "From Portland." He handed the teacher his schedule. Mr. Purvis read it over, then stared up at the two of them incredulously. "Kit Carson? *and*

Zachary Taylor?" His thick glasses magnified his piercing, beady eyes.

Finally, after what seemed like an eternity, the assistant principal managed to say, "All right, go on. You had better get to class."

"Thank you, sir," Kit and Zach both stammered, and they scampered up the rest of the stairs.

"Who was that?" Zach whispered as soon as they were safely on the second floor. "He's a scary guy."

"That was Mr. Purvis, the assistant principal in charge of discipline," Kit answered. "He *is* scary. We call him the Enforcer." She lowered her voice dramatically. "I've heard tales of kids who have gone into his office and never been the same. They wake up in the middle of the night, sweating and screaming his name."

"Oh, they do, do they?" Zach raised an amused eyebrow.

"Would I lie to you?" Kit asked, looking very innocent.

Zach studied her face for a second, then answered quietly, "No, I don't think you would."

The seriousness in Zach's voice caught Kit completely off guard. Suddenly she felt awkward and shy. "Um, why don't you show me your schedule now?" she blurted out, snatching the slip of paper from his hand. "You can tell a lot about a person from the classes he takes."

"You mean, like a fortune-teller?" Zach asked.

"Sort of, yes." Kit grinned impishly as her eyes ran down the page. "First of all, I know that you are new to our school and to Seattle, having just moved up here from Portland."

"Where does it say that?" Zach asked, peering curiously over her shoulder.

"It doesn't," Kit giggled. "You told me, remember?"

"Oh, right." Zach leaned against the wall and crossed his arms.

"You're a senior," Kit continued. "You have a keen interest in history, both American and European. You love to read. I see modern lit and Shakespeare. You're not too hot on math, but you don't mind a dash of science."

Zach nodded encouragingly, and Kit suddenly felt mischievous. She gasped dramatically and took a step back. "No wife is listed on the schedule."

"I certainly hope not!" Zach replied with a chuckle. "That would be real news to me."

"A girlfriend isn't listed, either," Kit went on, a bit more cautiously. "But it's hard to tell about that one." She raised her eyebrows questioningly.

"Nope." Zach shrugged. "No girlfriend."

Kit could hardly keep the pleased smile off her face, but the investigative-reporter instinct made her push the issue just a little further. "Not even a girl you left behind?"

"No." Zach shook his head emphatically.

Kit realized she might have gone too far and quickly brought the subject back to Zach's schedule. She lowered her glasses on her nose and stared hard at the paper. "I also see that you have a keen, observant eye. You like to watch the world at work and then report on it."

"How do you figure that?" Zach asked.

"You're taking journalism, and you volunteered to work on the *Spectator*," Kit replied with a grin.

"So is this where the party is?" A voice giggled from behind them in the hall. Kit knew before she even turned around who the intruder was: Molly Granby. Cute, perky, petite Molly.

"Hi, Molly," Kit said, trying not to show her lack of enthusiasm. "We're just recovering from a close encounter with Mr. Purvis."

"Ooh, isn't he terrible?" Molly said, wrinkling her turned-up nose. Then she focused her bright green eyes intently on Zach. "Kit," she said with a tiny pout, "aren't you going to introduce me?"

Usually Kit really liked Molly. When Molly was around guys, though, she transformed herself into a baby doll, playing the helpless little girl to the hilt. A lot of guys really fell for her act. Kit held her breath, hoping Zach wouldn't be one of them.

"Molly, this is Zach Taylor," Kit said, keeping a wary eye on Zach to gauge his reaction.

"Oh, so you're the new guy," Molly said in a breathy voice. "I've heard *all* about you."

"Hi," Zach replied politely.

When he didn't say anything else, Molly quickly asked, "So—you're from Portland?"

"Right." Zach jammed his hands into his pockets and swallowed hard.

"Do you like it here?"

"So far," he said with a nod. Then he looked over at Kit, an unmistakable plea for help in his eyes.

Kit was dumbfounded. Gone was the confident guy she'd been talking with just a few minutes earlier. In his place was an awkward, obviously uncomfortable boy whose eyes were darting from his shoes, to the ceiling, to the opposite end of the corridor.

"Zach's on the newspaper now," Kit offered

brightly, jumping into the conversation. "He's going to help whip the *Spectator* into winning shape."

"Great!" Molly said enthusiastically. Zach didn't pick up the ball, and the three of them stood there in silence.

"Well, I'd better get going," Molly said finally. "My hall pass says I only have ten minutes." The tiny redhead turned and bounced prettily down the hall. " 'Bye, Kit," she called over her shoulder, taking a second or two to peer back at Zach. "See you around, Zach."

"Sure," he replied, waving.

Kit smiled nervously at Zach and handed him his schedule, fully expecting him to shuffle off to his next class. Instead, he reached out and took hold of her right hand.

"Now it's my turn," he announced with a grin.

"What?" Kit said weakly. She was still stunned by the different Zach she'd just seen.

"To tell you your fortune," Zach explained.

"You know how to read palms?" Kit asked, forcing herself to look him in the eye. She was acutely aware of the pressure of his fingers against her palm.

"Sure," Zach replied with a straight face. "I studied at the same school of fortune-telling that you did." He led Kit over to the window

36

at the end of the hall, and the two of them leaned against the marble windowsill.

"I see that you are left-handed." Zach pointed to the ink on her fingertips. "And a bit accident prone."

Kit looked down at the red scar on her index finger where she had cut herself peeling potatoes a few weeks before. There were pencil-lead smudges along the base of her thumb as well. Kit suddenly felt very self-conscious about her hands.

"And, in tense situations," Zach continued, "you chew your fingernails to the bone."

"That's not fair!" Kit snatched her hand away and covered it with her other one. "You're supposed to read the *lines* in a person's palm, not the scars!"

"I'm getting to those." Zach reached out and cupped Kit's hands firmly in his. This time Kit felt a tingly sensation run all the way up her arm to her shoulder. Zach turned her palm up to study it more closely, and a beam of light blazed through the window onto her hand.

"I don't believe it!" Kit said, stepping back.

"What?" Zach said, sounding confused.

"The sun finally came out!" Kit gestured toward a shaft of light streaming into the hall.

"Do you realize that we've had three solid weeks of gray, and now this? It's wonderful!"

Zach was standing right in the middle of the pool of sunlight, grinning at her, and Kit caught her breath sharply. She had just opened her mouth to speak when the bell rang.

"Oh, no! Do you realize what we've done?" Kit cried. Zach shook his head. "Fifth period. It's completely over! We missed it."

They both stared wide-eyed at each other and then simultaneously shouted, "Who cares?"

Chapter Four

"It's happened!" Kit sang out as she burst through the front door of the Carson home that afternoon. The windows of the old Victorian house rattled as the door slammed behind her. "It's finally happened!"

Kit tossed her beret onto the standing brass coat rack in the hall and skipped through the kitchen into the family room. Her grandfather was sprawled comfortably in his easy chair in front of the television, engrossed in a movie.

Kit's parents were away on a much-needed vacation in Hawaii, so her grandfather was in charge of the house and taking care of Kit during their absence. Since he lived with the Carsons, anyway, life went on pretty much as usual.

"Gramps!"

He held up one hand, signaling Kit to keep silent for a minute. *Must be a western,* she thought. She shifted her attention to the flickering images on the television screen. Her grandfather could never be interrupted during a western.

She was right. John Wayne was just about to kiss Maureen O'Hara, silhouetted against a blazing sunset on the plains. The music swelled, the Big Kiss occurred, and Kit's grandfather hit the Pause button on the VCR with a satisfied slap. "Now, my dear, what's happened?"

"I met a boy!"

"That's incredible," her grandfather replied placidly, picking up the remote control and aiming it at the television once again.

"Wait a minute, Gramps!" Kit playfully swatted him on the arm. "This boy is special." She flopped down on the arm of his chair and put one hand on the old man's shoulder. "He seems to like me."

"And why shouldn't he?" her grandfather demanded. "Don't all the other boys like you?"

"You don't understand, Gramps. All the other guys *do* like me, but only as a friend. And this one . . ." Kit smiled at the sudden memory of Zach standing in that golden beam of light in the hall. "Well I think this one might be date material."

"Date?" Her grandfather sat up in his chair and switched off the VCR. "When?"

"Soon, I hope." Kit got up from the arm of the recliner and flopped down lengthwise onto the sofa. "He's new in school. I met him yesterday, and I talked to him today."

"Oh. So he hasn't asked you out?"

"Not yet," Kit admitted, then added brightly, "But I think he will!"

"Well, if he doesn't get around to it, don't feel too bad," her grandfather cautioned bluntly. "He probably has a lot on his mind."

"Gramps," Kit admonished, "I don't bruise *that* easily." She smiled warmly at the old man. He was so protective of her, in his own gruff, crusty way. Of course, he had seen her go through plenty of disappointments lately as far as guys were concerned.

The phone rang loudly, interrupting Kit's thoughts.

"I'll get it," she announced, springing off the couch and running toward the kitchen. In one swift movement she slipped the wall phone off its hook and hopped up on the stool by the kitchen counter.

"It's your quarter!" she sang merrily into the receiver.

41

"Hi, Kit!"

"Jessica," Kit said, recognizing her friend's voice, "I'm so glad you called!" Kit rummaged through the cabinet above her head until she found an open bag of cookies. "I wanted to tell you—"

"Did you find out if you'd be able to cover the tournament?" Jessica interrupted hurriedly.

"No, but I'm planning to bring it up on Monday in journalism." Kit took a bite of oatmeal cookie, then mumbled with her mouth full, "Hey, Jess, where are you?"

"I'm at practice. Coach Ericksen gave us a short break, so I'm in her office using the phone. I wanted to tell you that I can't see you this weekend. I've got to fit in some extra workouts. We do get Monday afternoon off, though."

"For good behavior?" Kit said, taking another bite of her cookie.

"Yeah, something like that." Jessica's laugh rang across the wire. "Listen, Kit, the reason I called is, I need your help."

Kit let out a hoot. "*My* help! What do *I* know about gymnastics? I can't even do a forward roll."

"No, silly!" Jessica giggled. "I saw this really gorgeous guy in school today, but I can't find out his name. I thought that you could help me out, since you always seem to know everything that's going on."

"What does he look like?"

"He's—" A shrill whistle overpowered Jessica's voice, and Kit had to hold the receiver away from her ear until it stopped.

"Oh, shoot, I've got to go," Jessica whispered. "Coach wants us back on the mats. Listen, if I don't see you at lunch on Monday, let's meet in the commons after school."

"In search of—the Mystery Man," Kit intoned mysteriously.

There was another ear-splitting whistle, and Jessica yelled, "Got to run! 'Bye!"

"Jessica, wait!" Kit shouted into the receiver, but a dial tone was her only response. Kit hung up the phone, disappointed that she hadn't been able to tell Jessica all about Zach. She grabbed another handful of cookies, popped one into her mouth, and munched slowly.

Maybe I'll have better luck this time if I keep my feelings to myself, she thought. Telling Jessica how she had felt about Jerry Gill certainly hadn't helped that potential romance!

Kit slid off the stool and stepped into the hallway. By the time she'd reached the foot of the stairs, she'd made up her mind to keep

Zach a special secret between herself and her grandfather.

As she passed the hall mirror, Kit glanced casually at her reflection. She looked like a real mess. There were bags under her eyes, and her hair was flying every which way. "Oh, no," she said, feeling panicky, "I'm going to see Zach again on Monday, and that leaves only two days to get ready!"

Kit ran straight upstairs to her bedroom and made a beeline for her nightstand. She scooped up the cloth-covered journal lying there and settled herself cross-legged on her bed. Grabbing a pencil, she flipped open the journal and began to make a list headed "Things to Do by Monday."

At the top of the list she wrote, "Give self oatmeal facial." The oatmeal usually ended up flaking all over the bathroom floor, but Jessica had highly recommended the treatment for girls with oily complexions. Kit had to admit she fell into that category.

Then Kit wrote, "Do fifty sit-ups in the morning and fifty before bed." She paused for a moment, then quickly changed the "fifty" to "ten."

"I don't want to be crippled by Monday," Kit muttered to herself. "Besides, exercise is something you have to ease into gradually."

Kit already planned to experiment with some new mascara and eye shadow that her mother had left behind. Saturday would be the perfect night for that. She and Gramps could watch a movie together, eat popcorn, and she might even paint her nails.

Under the category of "Wardrobe," Kit wrote: "Wash and iron clothes on Sunday. Decide on outfits for entire week."

Kit finished scribbling, hopped off the bed, and flung open her closet door. Monday's outfit would be the most important one of all. She held up a bright red skirt with a matching jacket that had huge padded shoulders. *No*, she told herself, putting it back, *too extreme.*

Kit spent the next hour trying to put together different ensembles, deliberating carefully over each one. None of them seemed quite right. *At this rate, I'll never make it to Friday*, she scolded herself.

She finally settled on a flattering black cotton jersey dress that draped loosely over her body.

Perfect, she thought, holding the dress up to herself in front of the mirror. "Since my exercise program won't have a chance to take effect by Monday, this will be more slimming."

Kit pulled a pair of matching black flats

from her closet and placed her black felt fedora beside the dress and shoes.

Finally she flopped down on her bed and heaved a satisfied sigh. She'd spend the whole weekend cultivating her natural beauty—and thinking about Zach.

From downstairs a barrage of gunshots sounded from the television, and John Wayne's voice hollered above the noise, "Charge!"

Chapter Five

Only one minute more, Kit told herself anxiously as she hurried down the hall after school on Monday. She hadn't caught a glimpse of Zach all day, but he was sure to be in the journalism room. At the classroom door, she paused just long enough to catch her breath and run a brush quickly through her hair. Then, flashing a big smile, she threw open the door—and froze.

Brian and Sam were working intently at their computer station, Melanie and Tony were going over notes at her desk, and Mr. Cunningham was thumbtacking suggestions for the next week's issue on the bulletin board. Zach was nowhere to be seen.

Kit's shoulders slumped, and she suddenly felt like crying. She'd spent the entire weekend preparing for her meeting with Zach, and now he wasn't even around. She dropped her bag to the floor with a clunk and let out an audible moan.

"Hey, Kit," Tony greeted her, pointing at her black dress, "who died?"

"Nobody died," she replied heavily. "I just thought I'd wear something different, something a little more dramatic, that's all." Before Tony could say another word, Kit snapped, "Anything wrong with that?"

Tony held up his hands and backed away. "Hey, no problem, Kit. Forget I said anything." Then he turned to Melanie and whispered loudly, "What's with her?" Melanie shrugged, looking equally bewildered.

"Sorry, Tony," Kit said, feeling foolish for letting her disappointment show.

"That's okay," Tony replied. "Just don't let it happen again!" he added with mock severity.

Kit mustered a half smile and slouched down at her desk.

"I see it's just the five of us once again," Mr. Cunningham said. "Well, let's get to work, folks. We've got a lot of ground to cover and not a lot of time to do it in."

The staff quickly pulled chairs into a circle and settled down to begin planning the next few issues of the *Spectator*. Kit noted miserably that there was still no sign of Zach. As though he were reading her mind, Tony remarked, "It appears that Mr. Taylor has decided to desert us—"

"Mr. Taylor is still trying to find his way around this labyrinth known as Queen Anne High," Zach interrupted, stepping into the room.

"Sorry, Zach," Tony said, looking a bit sheepish.

"No problem. Hi, everybody." There was a murmur of greetings, and Zach flopped easily into the empty chair beside Kit. "How's it going?" he asked her with a grin.

Kit felt her spirits lift right up out of the gloom. "Not bad," she answered, sitting up straighter and smoothing her hair to make sure it was in place.

"Attention, everyone!" Mr. Cunningham announced. "As you all know, the next three issues of the paper will be the ones we'll submit to the Scholastic Press Association for this year's evaluation. Needless to say, they'll have to reflect our best efforts. Last year the *Spectator* won the highest ranking in the state, and naturally, I'd like us to keep up the good work."

"Last year's good work was fueled by a full staff of hard workers, most of whom graduated," Melanie pointed out. "No offense to your editorship, Tony, but it's going to be twice as hard to match them with just a skeleton crew."

"Hey," Tony retorted, "what are we, chopped liver? Everyone in this room, except for Zach, of course, was a member of that team. There's no reason why, with a little extra work, we can't match last year's rating."

"Come on, Tony," Brian cut in tiredly. "Get serious!"

Before Tony could respond, Mr. Cunningham clapped his hands together loudly. "Ladies and gentlemen, I suggest we avoid letting this discussion degenerate into senseless bickering and stick to the real business at hand. The floor is now open for the introduction of new ideas. Anyone?"

"I have an idea!" Kit raised her hand.

"I thought you might, Miss Carson," Mr. Cunningham said, grinning. "Fire away!"

"Well, I found out on Friday that Jessica Finch will represent Queen Anne at the state invitational gymnastics tournament in Olympia."

"Way to go, Jess!" Tony called.

"And," she continued, "it just so happens that the meet is in three weeks. I thought that maybe each issue could focus on a stage of Jessica's preparation. First, on her training and background—you know, what led her to become a gymnast, how all those hours of practice fit into her life, and so on; then to her preparation here in Seattle; and finally on to the finals in Olympia."

"Where she's sure to win!" Melanie added.

"We could do a great photo spread," Tony said thoughtfully.

Kit nodded and dug into her bag. "I thought we might start with this picture. I took it on an old Instamatic when Jess was nine and first starting to take gymnastics."

Kit held up the snapshot of her best friend. Jessica was perched on the balance beam, trying hard to smile at the camera and maintain her poise at the same time. The combination of her youthful sweetness and determined concentration made the picture unforgettable. Kit had had it in her wallet for years.

Jessica carried a picture of Kit in her wallet, too. Kit had written a letter to their school paper in the second grade, and there she was, in the faded photo, proudly displaying the editorial page. They both carried more recent pictures of each other, of course, but these two were a secret joke between the two friends.

"She looks like a miniature ballerina," Zach said, leaning forward to take a closer look.

Kit felt a sudden pang of jealousy shoot through her.

"And look at this one," Melanie said, taking down a picture from the bulletin board. "It was taken last year at the sectional gymnastics competition." She flipped it over to Zach. "Isn't she beautiful?"

Zach whistled softly. "That's the understatement of the year."

The pang became a stab. Kit almost wished she'd never brought up Jessica at all.

"Ah, yes," Tony remarked, coming to stand behind Kit's chair. He peered at the pictures over her shoulder. "Queen Anne High's resident heartbreaker."

"Easy to see why," Zach said.

"But the best thing about Jessica is that she's not stuck-up at all," Melanie told him.

"Isn't it funny that she's never had a steady boyfriend." Tony shook his head.

"I find that hard to believe," Zach said, looking back at Jessica's picture.

Kit's spirits did a nose dive, and Tony joked, "Hey! Maybe she'll like Zach."

"Maybe," Melanie joined in. "A lot of boys are crazy about her, but she hasn't really gone for any of them. Zach here may be a different story, though."

"Cut it out, guys!" Zach protested, obviously embarrassed.

"Well, if you don't believe us," Melanie said, crossing her arms in front of her, "ask Kit. She knows all about Jessica Finch."

Suddenly Kit realized that all three of them were staring at her, waiting for her response. Trying desperately to remain casual, she flashed a big smile and said, "That's right. I am her best friend, and I do happen to know that she is very available."

Zach shot her a peculiar look. "Great," he said simply.

"Hey, is this a newspaper or a dating service?" Mr. Cunningham interrupted. "Let's get to work, people." He handed out a number of assignments and then said, "I think the feature on Jessica is a wonderful idea. Kit, since you and Zach did so well as partners last week, why don't you work on it together?"

"That would be fun," Zach replied, grinning at Kit. "I'd like that."

Kit looked into his clear blue eyes, and her heart started thumping loudly. "Terrific! We're an official team, then."

"Sure." Zach stuck out his hand and, they shook on the deal, sending a tingle all the way up Kit's right arm.

The rest of the time was devoted to planning other features and setting deadlines. Kit kept stealing glances at Zach, who would occasionally catch her at it and smile back.

"Okay, everybody, you have your assignments," Mr. Cunningham said. "Good luck!"

Brian and Sam mumbled their good-byes and disappeared quickly down the hall, with Melanie and Mr. Cunningham close behind them. Zach was busy reviewing his notes from the meeting, so Kit took her time putting her things back into her book bag. She could hear Tony clattering around in the darkroom, and she suddenly realized that she and Zach were alone. Kit racked her brain for something—anything—to say.

"Hey, I've got a great idea!" Tony announced, bursting out of the darkroom and shattering the silence. "Let's go celebrate your new partnership. I think we have the makings of a hot journalistic team here."

"I'm game," Zach said, standing up and sliding his notes into a manila folder. "How about you, Kit?"

She couldn't believe her good luck. "You bet!" Kit replied enthusiastically, slipping her book bag over her shoulder. Then she remembered her date with Jessica.

"Oh, wait a minute. I can't go," Kit moaned.

"I promised Jessica I'd do something with her this afternoon. I forgot all about it."

"So?" Tony replied. "Have Jessica come with us."

Kit hesitated. Normally, she knew Jessica would agree to a change in plans. But today was different. Today they were going to plan their manhunt for Jessica's mystery boy. Kit couldn't let her friend down.

"Did somebody call my name?" a voice trilled from behind them. Kit turned to find Jessica framed in the doorway. She looked stunning in her ruffled denim jumper and a crisp white linen shirt. Her hair was pulled into a thick blond braid down her back, and her skin seemed to be unusually glowing.

"Presenting Queen Anne High's number one sweetheart," Tony announced, using his pen as a microphone. "Ladies and gentlemen, may I present—Jessica Finch!"

With a laugh, Jessica pretended to take a bow. "How does anyone get any work done around here?" she said, straightening up. "You guys always seem like you're having too much fun to accomplish much of anything." Jessica gave Zach a friendly smile, then looked expectantly at Kit.

"Oh! I'm sorry!" Kit blurted out, remembering her manners. "Jessica, this is Zachary Taylor. He's new at Queen Anne."

"Hi, Zach." The room seemed to brighten perceptibly as Jessica smiled. Kit watched Zach blush deep red all the way to the roots of his hair.

Uh-oh, Kit thought glumly, *not him, too!*

"We were just talking about you," Tony said.

"Good things, I hope," Jessica replied cheerfully.

"Mr. C thought my series about you and the state invitational was a great idea," Kit informed her friend proudly.

"So you can come to the meet?" Jessica clapped her hands in delight. "That's wonderful!"

"And Zach here will be teaming up with Kit on the series," Tony added.

Jessica flashed Zach another dazzling smile.

"Tony suggested that we all go out and celebrate the series," Kit started to explain, "but I told him we'd made plans to—"

"Sounds great to me," Jessica cut in.

"But what about . . . ," Kit began lamely.

"Oh, *that* can wait," Jessica replied, dismissing Kit's objection with a wave. "Where should we go?"

A cunning gleam crept into Tony's eyes. "*I* think this occasion calls for a gelato at Truffaldino's on the waterfront."

"Tony is always looking for an excuse to have an Italian ice cream at Truffaldino's," Kit whispered loudly to Zach.

"That sounds terrific," Zach replied easily.

The group moved out into the hall and down the corridor toward the exit. Zach pulled open the big glass doors, and Kit stepped past him into the afternoon sunshine.

"Race you to the bus!" she said, feeling giddy with a sudden burst of happiness. "Last one there treats!"

Kit tore down the winding drive toward the city bus stop, keeping one hand on her head to hold on to her black hat. Zach ran beside her, laughing.

As they pounded down the road together, Jessica's and Tony's shouts of "Not fair! You guys cheated!" were lost in the wind.

Chapter Six

"Everybody off!" Tony cried suddenly and ran up the aisle toward the door of the bus. Kit, who was sitting between Zach and Jessica on the bench at the rear, glanced quickly out the window to check their location.

"Wait a minute!" she yelled. "We've got at least six more blocks to go!"

Tony ignored her and jumped off the bus, then turned and gestured frantically for them all to follow.

"Must be another one of his great ideas," Jessica murmured.

"If we don't get off right now," Zach pointed out, "Tony will be on his own for the rest of the afternoon."

Kit reached over and yanked the bell cord just as the driver began to close the doors and pull the bus away from the curb. He slammed on the brakes, and the rear exit opened with a *swoosh.*

"Thank you!" the trio chorused as they scampered off the bus and joined Tony. "Okay, wise guy," Kit demanded, "what's the big idea? We're nowhere near—"

"Quiet!" Tony raised one hand and cocked his ear toward the bay. "Listen to that!"

The only sound Kit heard was the whistle of a brisk salt breeze blowing up from the water. Zach looked perplexed. "I don't hear anything—"

"Wait! What's that?" Jessica broke in. "It sounds like the ringing of a ship's bell."

Tony nodded enthusiastically as the sound carried faintly up from the waterfront.

Kit's eyes widened. "The trolley!"

"Right!" Tony nodded. "And we have about two minutes to catch it."

Tony, Kit, and Jessica turned and started running as fast as they could down the hill toward the water.

"Wait a minute!" Zach yelled, scrambling to catch up. "Where are we going, anyway?"

"Just follow us!" came Tony's breathless reply.

They reached the green and yellow trolley with no time to spare. Tony and Zach battled each other to get on board first and claim a bank of seats for the four of them.

The conductor, dressed in an old-fashioned blue uniform with braided epaulettes, smiled wearily as Kit, Jessica, Tony, and Zach raced to the back of the car. There were only two other passengers, an elderly couple sitting toward the middle and snapping pictures out the window.

The brakeman rang the bright brass bell, and the trolley pulled slowly away down the track.

Tony began to sing "The Trolley Song." He was the only one who knew all the verses, so the others joined in on the chorus. Even the conductor perked up and rang his bell at the appropriate moments. The old couple applauded, and when they had finished the song Tony stood up and took a bow.

As the little trolley rattled along Alaskan Way, the broad street bordering the waterfront, Kit pointed out the sights to Zach.

"There's the *Princess Marguerite*," she said, gesturing toward a gleaming white steamship anchored in one of the slips. "You can take day trips on her to Victoria, Canada."

"We'll do that together this spring," Tony decided for them.

"Oh, we will, will we?" Zach asked, his blue eyes twinkling with amusement.

"Absolutely," Tony replied.

"Oh, there's the aquarium!" Kit cried. Zach craned his head to catch a glimpse of the blue-gray wooden structure to their right.

"They had the cutest baby sea otters there last spring," Jessica said. "I just love the way they float around on their backs, eating their food."

Zach chuckled. "Like little old men with moustaches, lounging around a swimming pool."

"End of the line!" the conductor announced as the trolley slowed to a stop.

"Come on!" Tony yelled, springing off the back of the tram onto the pavement. "Let's show Zach Ye Olde Curiosity Shoppe!"

He led them up to a weathered storefront covered with antique posters and hung with pieces of carved whalebone and Indian masks from Alaska. A fierce totem pole guarded the front entrance.

"So what do they have in this place?" Zach asked.

"The real question is, what *don't* they have," Tony replied, shoving open the door with his palm.

Kit had been hearing about the shop for

years, but she'd never gone inside. The over-
powering smell of musty old leather, sawdust,
and stale popcorn made her feel a bit nause-
ated. As her eyes adjusted to the dim light,
she noticed a vintage player piano in the corner. It was pounding out a faint, tinny rag-
time number, its ghostly keys moving up and
down by themselves along the keyboard.

"Why, there's just junk in here!" Kit said
disappointedly. She pointed to the long tables near the door which were laden with
tiny plastic totem poles and rubber Space
Needles.

"You're right," Jessica agreed, holding up
a dusty painted abalone shell. "Junky souve-
nirs."

"And old hunting trophies." Zach patted
the nose of a moth-eaten moose head hanging on one wall. "This guy has seen better
days."

A stuffed bear with big yellow teeth snarled
silently from the corner. Overhead, attached
to the broad wooden beams, hung all kinds
of animals—seals, sharks, otters, an albatross,
even a condor in full flight. From every corner and shelf drooped torn and knotted fish-
ing nets.

"You have to dig deep to find buried trea-
sure," Tony said mysteriously. "This stuff out

front is for tourists. They completely miss what's hidden in the back."

Tony led the way down the aisle toward the rear of the shop. Kit could vaguely make out some low glass cases in front of her, and for some reason she shivered. Suddenly Tony spun around and motioned for them to stop.

"My friends," he began in a low voice, "what you are about to witness is not for the faint of heart."

Instantly Jessica grabbed Zach's left arm.

Zach let out a yelp, and the two girls leapt back, startled. He turned to Jessica and grinned ruefully. "What are you trying to do, scare me out of my skin?"

Jessica giggled nervously. "Sorry, Zach," she said, "Tony's making me jumpy, that's all."

Tony pointed to a glass case with eyepieces positioned above each compartment. "Look into one of these magnifying glasses, and tell me what you see."

Zach, Kit, and Jessica exchanged glances, then followed his instructions. Kit approached hers and peered into the top of the glass case.

"Two fleas dressed up like a bride and groom," Kit declared, feeling relieved. "That isn't scary," she scoffed.

"And here's the Declaration of Independence, inscribed on the head of a pin," Zach said. "How'd they do that?"

Jessica mumbled something unintelligible.

"What is it, Jess?" Kit asked, concerned. "Are you okay?"

Jessica pointed to the case, her face pale. "Shrunken heads from the Amazon!" she said. "Real ones!"

Kit felt as if a cold, clammy hand had reached out and grabbed her neck. Her knees were definitely wobbling.

Zach reached out to steady her, and his touch shot through her body like a bolt of lightning. Kit jumped and bumped against the glass case with a loud crash.

"Hey, I won't bite, you know," Zach said, looking wounded.

"I know that," Kit answered, feeling embarrassed. "Those shrunken heads were really creepy."

"Oh, that's nothing," said Tony with an airy wave of his hand. "Wait till you guys see the mummy!"

"A real . . . ?" Jessica began.

"You bet!" Tony replied enthusiastically. "According to that sign on the display case, they found this guy about seventy years ago down in Death Valley."

Jessica looked ashen, but Tony babbled on. "They think he was an outlaw caught in an ambush, and he was shot through the side. The hot sand preserved the body perfectly. I mean, you can even see where the bullet went—"

"That does it!" Kit declared. "I'm out of here!"

Spinning on her heels, she wound her way stiffly through the aisles toward the exit. By the time she reached the door, Jessica was right behind her.

"I cannot *believe* Tony did that to us," Jessica grumbled as soon as they were out in the cool air. "That mummy was the grossest thing I've ever seen!"

"But, Jess," Kit pointed out, "we never actually *saw* the mummy."

"That's true," her friend admitted. "But I didn't have to see it. Those heads were bad enough. Yuck!"

"Hey, what's that?" Kit asked as a low moaning sound filled the air. She whirled around to see Tony and Zach lumbering toward them like Frankenstein monsters, their arms stretched out straight in front of them.

"Tony, you're pathetic!" Kit took off her hat and swatted him on the arm with it. "And, Zach, you're just as bad!"

66

Zach danced out of Kit's range, protesting, and she glared at him. "I'll get you later."

By now it was getting late, and they started up the hill to Truffaldino's for ice cream. A waitress seated them on the patio beneath a big red, white, and green umbrella, and fifteen minutes later they were savoring their cones.

Sitting directly across from Zach, Kit felt a lovely glow all over. *I could stay like this forever*, she thought happily.

The ice cream was making Kit thirsty, so she hopped up from the table and went over to the outdoor window. "Could I have a glass of water, please?" she asked the young girl behind the counter.

"Make that two!" Jessica chimed in, joining Kit beside the counter. Then she lowered her voice and whispered excitedly in Kit's ear, "Isn't he great?"

"Who?"

Kit started to turn around to scan the patio when Jessica clutched her arm. "Zach, silly. He's the guy I was talking about."

"Zach?" Kit felt her whole body go numb.

"I can't believe he's working with you on the newspaper," Jessica said with a giggle. "Talk about *luck*!"

"Zach," Kit repeated in a choked voice.

"Here's your water," chirped the girl behind the counter. Jessica thanked her, picked up one of the glasses, and hurried back to their table.

Kit focused her attention on picking up the other glass and then took a long drink. It was all she could do to keep from bursting into tears on the spot. She'd never have a chance with Zach if Jessica wanted him. Never.

Kit turned to look back at the trio beneath the umbrella. Jessica was laughing at something Zach had just said, and the lilting sound of her voice carried easily to Kit's ear. With a sharp pang she realized how great Jessica and Zach looked together. They were both blond, blue eyed, and incredibly attractive— the golden couple.

Kit shakily set down her glass spilling some of the water on the counter. Mumbling an apology to the girl, she forced herself to smile, then hurried back to the table.

"Listen, you guys," she said a bit too loudly, fixing her eyes carefully on Tony, "I forgot that I was supposed to be home fifteen minutes ago. Gramps is expecting me."

The others looked disappointed, but Kit hurried on, still keeping herself from looking directly at Jessica or Zach. "So I'll just run home. See you all tomorrow, okay?" Before her friends could respond, Kit backed away from the table and hurried toward the exit.

There was the scraping of chairs behind her, and she heard Zach call, "Kit, wait up! We'll go with you."

Just hearing him call her name made Kit's heart ache unbearably. Still keeping her back to the others, Kit called over her shoulder, "Sorry, I can't wait. 'Bye!" She gave a quick wave and headed toward the bus for home, feeling completely miserable.

Chapter Seven

"Oh, Gramps, the worst thing happened!"

Kit leaned heavily against the door jamb of the family room. Through the archway she could make out her grandfather's silhouette. He was obviously engrossed in another one of his movies.

"What's wrong?" her grandfather asked, peering around the side of the recliner. There was a click and a whir as the VCR was turned off.

"Jessica Finch is in love with Zachary Taylor."

Usually her grandfather would have greeted an announcement like that with a wisecrack, but instead he studied Kit's face intently. "Zachary, I take it, is the new boy you were talking about," he said finally.

71

"Yes." Kit felt her chin start to quiver, and she bit her lower lip to make it stop. "Of all the boys at Queen Anne High," she moaned, "why does Jessica have to take mine?"

"*Did* she take yours?"

"She might as well have," Kit replied bitterly. "All Jess has to do is look at Zach and he'll fall at her feet—just like all the other guys at school."

"Oh?" Her grandfather raised one eyebrow.

"It makes me so mad!" Kit slammed her hand against the wall. "I finally find someone I really like, a guy I even thought sort of liked me—and my best friend has to come along and grab him!"

As soon as the words were out, Kit wanted to take them back. She knew she wasn't mad at Jessica. She was angry with herself, for being such a failure with guys, and at life in general for being so unfair.

"Does Jessica know how you feel about this fellow?" her grandfather asked gently.

"Of course not." Kit sighed heavily. "Jess wouldn't go after him if she did. She's too good a friend."

"Then why don't you tell her about your feelings?"

"Oh, Gramps, you don't understand," Kit replied. "Zach is probably madly in love with her by now."

"Has he asked Jessica out yet?"

Kit shook her head.

Her grandfather cocked his head quizzically. "Then what are you worried about?"

Kit stared down glumly at her black flats and shrugged. How could she explain the situation to him?

"I just don't know about kids these days," her grandfather said with a sigh. "If I were a boy going to Queen Anne High School, I'd be beating a path straight to your door."

"Get serious, Gramps!" Kit rolled her eyes to the ceiling.

"I am serious!" He rubbed his chin, then shook one finger at her sternly. "You don't realize it, young lady, but you are very special. Unique! Any fellow with half a brain would see that."

Kit walked over to the recliner and solemnly kissed her grandfather on the bald dome of his head. "Thanks for trying, Gramps," she whispered. "But it doesn't help." She straightened up and moved toward the door. "I'll be upstairs until dinner," she said. "I need to think about things, okay?"

As Kit shuffled through the kitchen, the phone rang. Automatically she picked up the receiver. "I'm listening," she announced.

"Why is it that everybody else in the world

is content to use hello as a greeting, and you're not?" Jessica's voice demanded pleasantly.

Kit felt a twinge of jealousy hearing her friend's voice, but she quickly recovered. "I don't know," she answered, hopping up onto a stool.

"Was your grandfather mad?" Jessica whispered.

"About what?" Kit asked, puzzled.

"You seemed pretty upset when you left Truffaldino's," Jessica said, "about being late, and your grandfather, and—"

"Oh, that!" Kit suddenly remembered the excuse she'd made up to explain her hasty retreat from the ice-cream shop. "He was fine. He only yelled a little bit." She crossed her fingers behind her back.

"Well, I wish we'd all gone with you," Jessica said. "Guess who showed up right after you left?"

"Who?" Kit asked in a less-than-enthusiastic voice.

"Molly Granby!" Jessia replied. "I don't know how she found us, but she made such a big deal about what a coincidence it was that we all met up like that. And Zach and I were getting along so well—"

"What did Molly want?" Kit cut in.

"Zach, of course!" Jessica said. "She practically *threw* herself at him."

"You're kidding!" Kit suddenly got a vivid picture of Molly, coyly fluttering her eyelashes at Zach underneath one of Truffaldino's umbrellas.

"I mean, the way she was falling all over him, you would have thought he was her long-lost love," Jessica grumbled.

"'I thought she might have her eye on Zach," Kit said, remembering how Molly had acted in the hall at school.

"You bet she does," Jessica replied.

"Well, Molly won't have much luck with Zach. Not if she's competing against you, anyway." Kit sighed inwardly.

"I wouldn't be so sure about that," Jessica said hesitantly. "You know that steamroller look Molly gets on her face when she really wants something? Well, she was wearing it!"

"What did Zach do?" Kit asked.

"Well, he didn't say much. He just looked kind of embarrassed," Jessica replied. "In fact, he hardly said a word after you left."

"That girl makes me so mad!" Kit fumed.

"Gee, Kit," Jessica said, "It's not that big a deal, really."

"Yes, it is!" Kit declared. "Molly's not going to get her own way this time." Her sense of despair over Jessica and Zach seemed to evaporate as she focused her frustration on Molly.

"What are you going to do?" There was a touch of nervousness in Jessica's voice.

Kit paused for a moment, took a deep breath, and quickly went over the situation in her head.

It was really very simple. She and Zach weren't going to be together. She'd seen the way he'd reacted to Jessica's picture, how flustered he'd been when he first met her, and how much fun they'd had together at the waterfront. The signs were all there. It was just a matter of time before they'd be going out—unless Molly Granby got her way.

The thought of Zach falling into Molly's clutches made Kit furious, no matter how slight that chance was. If *she* couldn't have Zach for a boyfriend, Kit wanted Jessica to be the lucky one. And, anyway, if she made sure that Zach and Jessica fell in love, at least she would still have Zach as a friend. Romance and Kit Carson just weren't compatible. Besides, in the long run, friendships lasted longer.

"I'm going to see to it that you and Zach get together," Kit said firmly.

"How are you going to do that?" Jessica asked, an edge of uncertainty in her voice. "I don't even know for sure if he likes me."

"Zach likes you, all right," Kit assured her

friend. "He's just shy, that's all." Kit bit her lip and thought for a moment. "I've got it!" she said, snapping her fingers. "The article for the *Spectator!* That'd be a perfect place to start."

"Are you sure about this?" Jessica asked.

"Absolutely. I'll have Zach handle the interview with you. That way you'll have to spend some time together, getting to know each other. . . ." Kit felt a sudden pressure in her throat, but she took a deep breath and continued. "Molly won't have a chance."

"That'd be terrific!" Jessica said enthusiastically. "You really are a great friend!"

"Yeah, that's me," Kit replied, trying to sound cheerful. "Always a bridesmaid, never a bride."

There was a startled silence on the other end. "What do you mean by that?" Jessica asked finally.

"It means that you and Zach will be getting together," Kit said brightly. "And I'll be right there, cheering you guys on."

After she hung up the phone, Kit slumped against the kitchen cabinet. Now she, Kit Carson, was the official matchmaker for Jessica Finch and Zachary Taylor.

Chapter Eight

The next day a very different Kit strode into the journalism classroom. She had a look of firm resolve in her eyes and felt a sense of renewed purpose. She had promised Jessica she'd help her get the boy of her dreams, and once Kit Carson decided to do something, she went at it wholeheartedly.

"Hey! Where is everybody?" Kit called from the doorway. The classroom was deserted.

"I guess it's just you and me today!"

"What?" Kit peered around the door to see who had spoken, and her heart skipped a beat.

Zach was sitting on Mr. Cunningham's desk, his long legs dangling off the side, looking more handsome than ever. Kit took a deep breath and reminded herself to stay level-headed.

"Where are Mr. Cunningham and the Hardy Boys?" she asked, referring to Sam and Brian. "And Tony and Mel?"

"Well, let's see. . . ." Zach crossed his arms over his chest and grinned. "Mr. C went to talk to Mr. Purvis about the invisible staff."

"It's about time," Kit said emphatically, setting her book bag on her desk. "Purvis will scare them back to work."

"Brian and Sam went to a computer fair, and Melanie's out selling advertising," Zach continued. "Tony's photographing the Glee Club since he can't make it to their performance tomorrow night."

"Why not?"

Zach shrugged. "He said he had a conflict."

Kit hooted derisively. "That's what *he* says!" Zach shot her a curious look and Kit explained, "The Glee Club is notorious for their endless concerts." She closed her eyes and faked a loud snore.

"I see." Zach chuckled. "And the only people who ever make it to the end are their devoted parents."

"You got it." Kit settled into a desk across from Zach.

"We had the same problem down in Portland, only with the school orchestra." He grimaced at the memory. "Used to avoid it like the plague."

As they laughed, Kit couldn't help noticing how vibrant his blue eyes were. They were flecked with gold and twinkled in the light.

"Well!" Zach slid off the desk and sat down next to Kit. "How should we begin?"

"Begin what?" Kit murmured. She was still mesmerized by his eyes.

"The Jessica Project."

His mentioning Jessica brought Kit back to reality. She reminded herself that the whole situation would be easier if she kept a businesslike attitude.

"I thought we could approach it simply," Kit began, rummaging in her purse for a pen. "You know—past, present, and future."

Zach nodded. "Since you're Jessica's best friend, I think you should handle the past part." He idly flipped a pencil in the air, catching it easily.

"My thoughts exactly." Kit scribbled a brief note on her trusty yellow pad. "I think you should make a date to talk to Jessica about what she's doing now to prepare for the tournament."

"Date?" Zach's voice broke comically over

the word. Then he blushed, cleared his throat, and repeated more levelly, "Date?"

"Yes." Kit nodded.

"Oh, no," Zach muttered. "I couldn't do that."

Kit couldn't understand his hesitancy. Was it because he *didn't* want to go out with Jessica? She forced herself not to get her hopes up.

"Why not?" Kit asked, holding her breath.

"For one thing, she'd turn me down."

"Oh." Kit exhaled the word.

"Besides," he added, "I don't even know her."

"You sound just like Jessica," Kit said, feeling a little exasperated. "How can you get to know someone unless you ask her out?"

"There are lots of ways!" Zach countered, looking a little flustered. "You say hello in class, or in the halls. You work on a project together—"

"So it's perfectly reasonable for you to ask her out," Kit interrupted. "And tell her you'd like to interview her."

There was a moment's silence as Zach stared out the window. Kit realized that he was basically a shy person who needed a little prodding.

He spun around abruptly and asked, "Are

we talking about a full-fledged, drive-to-her-house, go-out-to-dinner-and-a-movie kind of date?"

"Well," Kit said casually, "if you don't feel comfortable with that, you can ask her out for a go-for-a-Coke-at-the-sub-shop interview."

"I think I'd be more comfortable with that," Zach said firmly, still sounding worried.

"You act as if dating is torture."

"Well, it is in a way. I've never been very good with girls," Zach confessed. "I mean, I've had girlfriends, of course, but this dating stuff, it's so formal and artificial—I wouldn't know what to say."

"I don't believe that for a minute!" Kit smiled encouragingly. "You do just fine when you talk to me."

"You're different."

Kit's smile disappeared. He might just as well have said she was ugly.

"Boy," Kit muttered, "if I had a dollar for every time a boy has said that to me, I'd be a millionaire."

"Come on, Kit, you know what I mean!" Zach said. "You're on the newspaper staff. We have a lot in common, like the same things, laugh at the same jokes. I mean, I feel like I've known you my whole life."

To Kit, Zach's words only seemed to emphasize the fact that they would never be more than just friends. Kit felt tears stinging her eyes and swallowed hard, forcing herself to smile.

"But Jessica!" Zach continued. "What would we ever find to talk about?"

Kit knew she had to do something or she really would cry. "Look," she said suddenly, "why don't you pretend I'm Jess for a minute? I'll prove to you that there's lots you can talk about."

Zach hesitated, considering the suggestion. Then a tiny smile crept across his face. "Okay," he said, "we'll try it." He moved quickly to the classroom door, leaned out, and checked both ways down the hall. "But, if anyone comes by, let's stop, okay?"

"I promise." Kit placed a hand across her heart. "Now, you sit in Mr. C's chair. His desk can be a restaurant table." She pulled another chair up to the desk directly across from Zach and took a deep breath. "Okay. Ready?"

Zach nodded and cleared his throat noisily. "Ready."

Kit straightened her back into Jessica's perfect posture, delicately rested her chin on her hand, and looked into Zach's eyes.

"I'm glad we came here, Zach." She pitched

her voice like Jessica's—high and slightly breathy. "The Seattle Scoop is one of my favorite places."

"I like it, too." Zach paused.

Kit smiled at him encouragingly. He swallowed nervously and said, "You know, it kind of reminds me of the local hangout at my old school."

"Oh?" Kit replied. "Where was that?"

"Portland."

Kit nodded, waiting for him to continue.

"In Oregon."

Kit giggled, and Zach shook his head and grumbled, "This isn't easy, you know."

"You're doing just great," Kit said encouragingly. "Now, don't break character!" Zach grinned and nodded.

"So tell me about this hangout," she prodded.

"Well, it was called Nick's," Zach began. "Nick is Greek and makes the best gyros in the world." A warm light crept into his eyes at the memory. "Actually, most of us met there for breakfast."

"You're kidding! Breakfast?"

"Yeah, it's pretty amazing, but everybody got up a full hour earlier, just to chow down on Nick's great hash browns."

"Was the food really that good?"

"I think it had more to do with old Nick

himself. He was some guy." Zach leaned back comfortably in his chair. "He'd always ask us about what we were doing. And we'd complain about upcoming tests, deadlines, whatever. And he would always give us the same advice." Zach grinned and, wagging his finger at her, said with a heavy accent, "Study! Study! Study!"

Kit giggled and leaned her chin on her hands as Zach continued.

"Nick always found time to listen to a problem, no matter how busy he got. We all knew we could count on him."

"That's a good friend."

"You know," Zach said, leaning forward earnestly across the desk, "now that I think about it, I bet Nick was responsible for a lot of kids staying in school, ones who might have given up and dropped out."

"Zach, that would make a great story!" Kit enthused, the journalist in her bubbling up to the surface. "Did you ever try to write it up?"

He shook his head. "But I'd like to." Zach ran his hand through his hair. "I haven't even thought about Portland for a while. I guess I've been concentrating on fitting in here."

"If I may say so," Kit said warmly, "you're really doing well."

"Thanks." Zach's eyes held hers for just a moment, then he quickly looked away. "Jessica."

His reminder caught her by surprise. Kit had forgotten all about their playacting, but she recovered quickly. "See how easy it is?"

Kit turned her attention to stuffing her note pad into her book bag, hoping Zach wouldn't see the pink in her cheeks. She heard his chair scrape back from the desk, and when Kit looked at him again, he was standing up.

"Gee," Zach said, a relieved grin on his face, "if the real date with Jessica goes as smoothly as the practice one, it could be fun."

"Great!" Kit said with forced enthusiasm. Then a faint knocking at the door caught their attention. "Come in," she yelled.

The door swung open, and a dark-haired stranger peered around the corner. "Is Kit Carson in . . . ?" the strikingly handsome boy started to ask.

"Burke!" Kit shrieked, leaping out of her seat and running to meet him. She flung her arms around his neck and hugged him tight. "Gosh, it's good to see you!"

"I've been trying to track you down for the

last hour," Burke said, an excited grin on his face.

"I'm glad you found me!" Kit looped her arm in his, then remembered that Zach was there. She turned and said, "Oh, Zachary, I want you to meet my friend, Burke Walker." The two boys shook hands briefly as Kit rattled on, "Burke's a senior across town at Garfield High."

"Uh, Kit, can I talk to you a minute?" Burke asked shyly. He gestured toward the hall and added "In private?"

"Sure!" Kit smiled up at her friend. Burke had lived next door to Kit until junior high, when his parents bought a new house over near Lake Washington. Even though they didn't see each other very often, they were still good friends.

As soon as they were outside the door, Burke turned to Kit and said very seriously, "I wanted you to be the first to know. I got accepted to MIT today."

Before Kit could smother him with another hug, Burke held up his hand and said, "*And* —so did Rhonda!" This time he picked Kit up and spun her around.

"Oh, Burke, that is so fantastic!" Kit gasped. Rhonda White was Burke's girlfriend who still went to Queen Anne High.

"Mind if I break the news in my column?" Kit inquired. "It would be a great item!"

"If Rhonda doesn't mind," he replied, blushing furiously. "I mean, it's her school paper." He checked his watch and said, "Hey, I'd better run. Rhonda's waiting for me out front."

Kit waved as she watched her friend saunter down the hall. With a touch of wistfulness, she thought back to those three months in her sophomore year when her friendship for Burke had advanced to a crush. But Burke had been too busy falling in love with Rhonda at the time to notice. Of course, once Kit had realized what was going on, she had been instrumental in bringing the two of them together.

Now it was happening again. One good friend helping another. Jessica Finch, meet Zachary Taylor, courtesy of Kit Carson.

When she stepped back into the journalism room, Zach was standing by the window, looking thoughtfully into the distance.

"Special friend of yours?" he asked lightly, turning at the sound of her step.

"Very special!" Kit replied, thinking back to how long she and Burke had been friends.

Something made her glance quickly up at Zach. He was looking at her in a peculiar way, almost as if she had said something wrong.

"Zach? Are you okay?"

Just as quickly the look disappeared, and he was his normal self. "Hey, if I'm going to arrange a date with Ms. Jessica Finch"—he grinned—"I'd better get cracking."

"Let's go to the gym," Kit said, checking her watch. "Practice should be close to breaking up."

Zach was out of the room before she finished speaking.

Kit still hoped against hope that he might secretly like her. She felt a sharp pain as the door swung shut.

Zach likes Jessica, Kit told herself matter-of-factly. *And that's all there is to it.*

Chapter Nine

On Thursday morning Kit woke up with a start. A strange, quivery feeling was gripping her insides. She squinted at the brilliant sunlight streaming in through her bedroom window and tried to collect her thoughts.

Jumbled images and snippets of conversation floated through her mind. Zach, his hands jammed in his pockets, his head down, talking to Jessica in the gym. Jessica, nodding shyly, her eyes focused on the parquet floor of the gym. The phone, ringing loudly. Jessica's voice asking, "Are you sure my blue knit dress isn't too dressy?" Her own voice answering, "Wear jeans if it makes you more comfortable."

For the last twenty-four hours Kit had been focusing all her energy on some important upcoming event—but what *was* it? She shook her head groggily, then bolted straight up in bed.

"Today's their first date!"

Just mentioning the fact out loud filled Kit's stomach with butterflies. Throwing back the quilt on her yellow cast-iron bed, she scurried across the floor to her dresser. She found her glasses, slipped them on, and quickly glanced at her clock.

"Seven! Oh, no!" Kit took a look at herself in the mirror and gasped. Staring at her was a puffy-eyed girl in a blue and white-striped nightshirt, with wire-framed glasses perched precariously on her nose and a bird's-nest hairdo.

"I'll never be ready in time," Kit muttered, dashing across the hall to the bathroom. After quickly washing and blow-drying her hair, slapping on a dash of makeup, and trying on three different outfits, Kit bolted for the kitchen. It was now almost seven-thirty. She'd agreed to meet Zach on the school steps at eight for a last-minute pep talk.

"Hey, where's the fire?" her grandfather called from over his morning paper. Kit popped two pieces of bread into the toaster and poured herself a glass of orange juice from the refrigerator. "Today's the big date," she mumbled between sips.

"Well, good luck!" Her grandfather looked her up and down and beamed proudly. "I think you look swell!"

"Thanks, Gramps, but it's not my date."

"Not yours?" he said, sounding confused.

"No." Kit sprinkled some cinnamon on her toast and took a loud, crunchy bite. "It's Jessica's."

"Oh." Her grandfather scratched his head, then shrugged. "Well, then, wish *her* luck!"

"I will." Kit rinsed out her glass in the sink and headed for the back door.

"Now, hold on a minute!" her grandfather commanded. "If it's Jessica's big date, what's it got to do with you?"

"I'm going to make sure it all runs smoothly," Kit explained.

"Oh." He paused. "And who is the lucky young man?"

"Zachary Taylor," Kit answered, trying to keep her voice calm.

"*Your* Zachary Taylor?" Her grandfather persisted.

"He's not mine, Gramps," Kit answered quickly. "He likes Jess, not me."

Before her grandfather could ask any more questions, Kit pulled her straw hat off the brass coat rack and blew him a kiss. "See you later, Gramps!" she called, sailing out the door.

"I feel ridiculous," Zach grumbled as Kit greeted him in front of the school.

"Why? You don't look ridiculous." Kit adjusted her glasses and peered at him closely. Zach looked wonderful, as far as she was concerned. She fought back a sharp pang of longing.

"I woke up at five o'clock this morning because I was so nervous about this thing with Jessica."

"It's called a date," Kit corrected. "And you shouldn't feel stupid. Everybody gets nervous."

"That's not what's bothering me." Zach shook his head. "I must have tried on five different shirts this morning, trying to find one I thought Jessica might like."

"The one you're wearing is fine," Kit assured him. It was a collarless pale blue shirt that intensified his electric-blue eyes. "You look very nice."

"Thanks." He relaxed visibly and smiled. "I finally decided that there was no way I could guess what she likes, anyway."

"Well, you guessed right," Kit said. "Blue is Jessica's favorite color."

"Hey, what do you know! I did something right." Zach looked at Kit curiously. "What's yours?"

"Red." Kit gestured to her oversize red shirt and red flats.

"I should have guessed." Zach grinned appreciatively. "That color looks good on you."

"Thanks," Kit replied, blushing at his compliment. She fumbled for a piece of paper in her bag and pressed it into Zach's hand.

"What's this?" he asked.

"I made up a list of questions you should ask Jessica." As a stricken look came over Zach's face, Kit added hastily, "In case you run out of things to talk about, I mean."

Zach tucked the note into his shirt pocket and stared down at his feet. "Now I feel doubly stupid."

"I'm sure you won't need the list," Kit said encouragingly. "These questions are more for the newspaper, you know."

"Right, right." Zach nodded, shifting his weight restlessly. "You'd think I'd never talked to a girl before."

"You'll do just fine," Kit said, reaching out to pat his arm.

"I mean, it's not like it's a big date, or anything," Zach said anxiously.

"No, no," Kit agreed. "You're just going out for a soda and a little light conversation."

Zach took a deep breath and exhaled deeply. "It's no big deal." He backed away toward the entrance to the school, nearly tripping over a big stone planter on the sidewalk. He turned and called over his shoulder, "Wish me luck!"

Zach looked so vulnerable that Kit felt almost like hugging him. Knowing that he probably wouldn't want to hug her back only made her feel worse. With a sigh, Kit forced herself to head for her first class. It was going to be a long day.

By the time Kit met Jessica at lunch, her friend was in almost as bad shape as Zach.

"How do I look?" Jessica whispered anxiously. She had decided to wear the knit dress after all. It was sea blue and showed off her figure beautifully. Kit felt clunky standing beside her.

"You look as if you just stepped out of a fashion magazine," Kit replied truthfully.

"I'm a little nervous about this date with Zach," Jessica confessed. "I didn't realize until this morning that I've never really been alone with him."

"It'll only be for half an hour," Kit said. "Don't you have to go to practice today?"

"Yeah. All the same, Kit, I wish that you were going to be there with me."

"I'd just be in the way," Kit said. "Besides, I have to interview the chess club president."

Jessica looked confused "I didn't even know we *had* a chess club at Queen Anne."

"You see?" Kit said, throwing her arms up helplessly. "That's exactly why we need this article! No wonder the club's membership has dropped to one person."

Jessica narrowed her eyes suspiciously. "Kit, are you kidding me again?"

"*Moi?*" Kit asked. "How could you even think such a thing?"

Jessica swatted her friend. "This all better go right."

"It'll be fine," Kit said, beginning to feel like a broken record.

"But what will Zach and I *say* to each other?" Jessica bit her lip.

"Well, what do you talk about with other guys when you're not on a date?" Kit asked.

Jessica shrugged. "School, sports—"

"Then talk about those!" Kit draped her arm around her best friend's shoulders. "Look, Zach's a great guy, and he's really easy to talk to. You won't have to worry about a thing, believe me."

"I sure hope so." Jessica still sounded unconvinced. Suddenly the bell rang, and Jessica backed hurriedly toward the steps. "I'll talk to you tonight," she called. "Wish me luck!"

Kit watched, dumbfounded, as Jessica nearly tripped over the same stone planter that Zach had barely avoided that morning.

Chapter Ten

After school Kit sat in one of the big red booths at the Seattle Scoop and tried to concentrate on what Tony was saying. Her mind wandered as she nervously scanned the restaurant, looking for Jessica and Zach.

"Kit, are you listening to me?" Tony waved his hand in front of her face to get her attention.

"Huh?" Kit snapped to and focused on her friend. "What did you say?"

"I said," Tony repeated, exaggerating his words, "you haven't heard a thing I've said for the last five minutes."

"I have, too!" Kit lied. "Uh, Tony, what time do you have?"

"It is now three forty-six," he answered without even checking his watch. "Exactly one minute later than the last time you asked. What are you waiting for, anyway?"

"Nothing." Kit reached out and grabbed a french fry off Tony's plate. "It's just that Jessica was going to meet Zach here this afternoon, and I don't see either one of them. They're supposed to be doing an interview for the paper."

"Speaking of which," Tony said, pounding the bottle of catsup with his fist, "Mr. Cunningham told me that Purvis is planning to meet with the entire *Spectator* staff on Monday."

"The entire staff?" Kit repeated, her eyes widening. "You mean, the invisible ones will be there, too?"

"Yep. Jerry Gill and the rest of his gang are going to be told they have to shape up or ship out."

"Well, I hope Mr. Purvis calls in Coach Colacci, because he's a big part of the problem."

"Yeah, Colacci's going to be there," Tony said, sipping his soda. "And Ms. Ericksen."

"That should be exciting!" Kit reached for a whole handful of Tony's fries. "Brain versus brawn!"

Tony slipped off the cushioned seat and dropped some change on the table. "I've got to get moving. By the way, Zach and Jess are here." He pointed to a booth across the aisle just behind Kit.

"Tony!" Kit practically shouted. "Why didn't you *tell* me?"

"I forgot," he replied, ducking as Kit threw her napkin at him. "Listen, I've got an article to finish, okay? I'll call you later."

After Tony had left, Kit leaned back and glanced casually over the top of the booth. Across the aisle she could see Jessica and Zach clearly. They obviously hadn't noticed her.

Both of them looked a little nervous. Kit watched as Zach searched for something, patting his shirt pocket several times, and then finally discovered the pen in his spiral note pad. Jessica tucked her blond hair behind one ear, waiting patiently. Loud music was blasting from the jukebox in the corner, so Kit couldn't catch any of their conversation.

Instinctively she slumped way down in her booth and craned her neck around the side so she could hear better.

What am I doing? Kit thought. *This is spying. I should leave.* She pulled her head back in and started to gather her belongings. *Now, wait a minute,* another voice in her mind scolded, *concern for your friends' welfare is not spying.*

101

Kit felt that that voice had a point, and she made up her mind to stay just a tiny bit longer.

Suddenly the music stopped, and Kit heard Zach say, "So, uh, Jessica—"

Kit cringed a little in her seat as she heard the telltale crinkle of paper being unfolded. Zach was already having to resort to the list of questions she'd given him. The date was turning into a full-fledged interview, after all.

"So, are you nervous about the tournament?" Zach asked.

"A little," Jessica replied. "I guess I'm always scared before a meet."

"Yeah. I can understand that."

"Oh, are you into sports, too?" Jessica asked brightly.

"No," Zach replied simply.

"Oh."

There was an awkward silence before Zach continued, "But I can imagine how nervous I'd get."

There was another pause.

"That is, if I were involved," Zach added lamely. "Which I'm not."

"Right."

The jukebox started up again, and the rest of the conversation was drowned out by the music. Kit couldn't believe how formally Zach and Jessica were acting. Where was the easy-going, wisecracking Zach she knew? And the confident, ever-sparkling Jessica? Kit raised her head cautiously to peer over the top of the booth.

Zach was staring intently at his drink. Jessica's face was frozen in a half smile, and she was twirling a strand of hair around one finger.

Is that how lovestruck couples behave? Kit asked herself. *Maybe I'd better find out if something's gone wrong.* Quickly grabbing her book bag, Kit slipped off the seat and crept out of sight around the far side of the booth. Then she straightened up and walked back toward Jessica and Zach as if she'd just come in.

"Hey, you guys!" Kit called, "How's it going?"

Jessica and Zach greeted her with a pair of big, relieved smiles.

"Kit!" Zach scooted over to make room for her in the booth. "Sit down."

"Oh, I don't want to intrude or anything," Kit protested.

"You're not." Jessica pointed at the empty space and ordered, "Sit."

As Kit slid onto the seat, Zach was already motioning to the waitress. "I'll buy you a soda," he offered.

"Great," Kit replied. "I'm dying of thirst." There was no point in mentioning that she was already oversaturated with soda. "Hey, what happened to this straw?" she asked, lifting a crumpled, knotted piece of red- and white-striped plastic and dangling it in front of Zach's nose.

"I'm in training for my Scout merit badge," he said seriously.

"They give badges for straw knotting?" Kit shot him a dubious look.

Jessica giggled, and Zach leaned back against the side of the booth, smiling impishly. "Sure," he replied.

The waitress brought Kit's Coke, and Jessica said, "Zach and I were just talking about my gymnastics meet. I was telling him how nervous I always get."

"Yeah, you do," Kit said. "But you always look as cool as a cucumber."

"I'm the complete opposite," Zach said with a chuckle. "Whenever I have to talk in front of a group, my throat goes dry and my knees lock."

Kit nodded sympathetically. "For as long as I can remember, my teachers have always made me erase the blackboard before I gave a report for the class."

"Why?" Zach asked, looking puzzled.

"Because I get so nervous that my hands shake," Kit explained. "I guess erasing the board was supposed to settle me down."

Jessica giggled again. "Remember that time you brought your collection of little glass animals to show-and-tell in fifth grade?"

"Oh, yeah!" Kit rolled her eyes. "Mrs. Blanton was so afraid I'd drop them that she made me point each one out with a ruler."

"So you had to give up your plans of becoming a brain surgeon," Zach quipped.

"Yeah, what a tragedy!" Kit replied, laughing. "But I've decided to go for Ph.D. in blackboard cleaning. I've already put in plenty of training."

"Coach Ericksen is going to make me do more than erase boards if I don't get to practice," Jessica said suddenly, looking at her watch. "She's called in a special trainer from the university to help me out." She pulled her gym bag out from beneath the table and stood up. "Listen, Zach, thanks for the soda. I hope you got enough material for your interview."

Zach winced. "I don't know. I may have to have Kit—"

Kit cut him off. "We'll just have to set up another session for you guys. Okay, Jess?"

Jessica shrugged pleasantly. "Sure, Kit.

Whatever you say. Hey," she added, "why don't you two come and watch me work out tomorrow? Coach Ericksen said we could invite a few people. You know, to perform in front of an audience."

"Sounds great!" Zach said enthusiastically.

Kit nodded. "We'll bring Tony along to photograph you."

After Jessica's lithe figure had disappeared out the door of the soda shop, Kit turned to Zach and asked cheerfully, "Well, how'd it go?"

Zach didn't answer. Instead, he put his hand over his eyes and slid slowly under the table.

"It was awful!" Jessica groaned to Kit over the phone that evening. "We just sat there like lumps."

"What went wrong?" Kit asked carefully, feeling her heart quicken. In spite of everything, part of her was hoping that Jessica would say she didn't like Zach anymore.

"I'm not sure," Jessica replied. "I mean, I expected Zach to be like he was at the waterfront that day, but he just clammed up as soon as we sat down."

"He probably needed a little time to loosen up, that's all," Kit reassured her.

"Yeah, well," Jessica muttered, "we'd hardly said ten words to each other before you came along, anyway."

Kit froze at her friend's reproachful tone. Did Jessica think she had ruined her date?

"Wow, I'm sorry, Jess," Kit said. "I should have left you guys alone. It won't happen again, I promise."

"No, no, don't worry about it," Jessica said hurriedly. "It was a good thing you joined us, or we'd probably still be sitting there, staring at each other."

After they'd hung up, Kit sat for a moment by the phone. With a sinking feeling, she realized that Zach and Jess probably would have gotten along just fine without her.

"Two's company," she announced to the empty kitchen. "And three is definitely a crowd."

Chapter Eleven

The next day Kit met Tony outside the entrance to the school gym. Tony was carrying his Nikon camera, with electric flash attached, and two light meters dangled from his neck. A red nylon camera bag, bulging with extra lenses and accessories, bounced off his right hip as he walked.

"Tony, I only need a couple of pictures of Jessica in action," Kit said, grinning as her friend struggled to keep his gear together. "You look as if you're going on a major fashion shoot!"

"Be prepared, that's my motto," Tony said cheerfully. "A truly great photojournalist is always ready for anything." He checked the top of the camera, then dug anxiously into the bag.

"And what did the truly great photojournalist forget?" Kit asked sweetly as Tony began ransacking the bag again.

He looked up and gave Kit a sheepish grin. "Film," he said. "I must have set it down someplace while I was packing all this stuff." He slapped himself on the forehead. "How could I be so stupid?"

Kit checked her watch and grimaced. "Oh, boy. Jessica said she'd be running through her floor routine right at three-thirty."

"That leaves us five minutes," Tony said, glancing at his own watch. He squeezed his eyes shut in concentration. "Now, where could I have left that stupid film?"

"Maybe Mr. C has an extra camera in his office, or at least an extra roll of film," Kit offered hopefully.

Tony shook his head. "That's the roll I took."

"Why don't you try Kit's surefire memory method?" a voice suggested from behind them. Kit's face lit up as she turned to find Zach sauntering down the hall. He flashed a warm smile in her direction.

A flood of mixed emotions charged through Kit. She was thrilled to see Zach and flattered that he'd remembered her memory dance. At the same time, she felt guilty for being so thrilled and flattered. *He's Jessica's boyfriend*, she reminded herself, *or at least he will be.* Hurriedly she turned her attention back to Tony, hoping that Zach couldn't read her face.

"Quick, Tony," she ordered, "go through the motions of how you got the film, picked up the bag—everything!"

Tony stared at her as if she had lost her mind.

"I'm serious! It really helps." Kit consulted her watch again, then changed tactics. "Look, Roman, if you don't try it, we're going to have a huge, blank space on the front page of the *Spectator*, and you'll have no one to blame but yourself!"

"Okay, okay." Tony shut his eyes and began to mime his previous actions. "Let's see, I got the bag off the shelf," he muttered. "Then I picked up my pack from the desk, put on the light meters . . ." His voice trailed off as he opened his eyes and noticed a few passing students whispering among themselves and pointing in his direction. Even Zach was obviously having a hard time not laughing.

"Keep going!" Kit said sternly. "We've only got two minutes left, and you haven't gotten to the film part yet."

"Boy, is she strict," Tony complained to Zach. "I really feel like an idiot."

"Don't worry," Zach replied. "You don't look half as silly as Kit did when I caught her doing her memory dance."

Kit stuck her tongue out at Zach, and he chuckled.

"Okay, so I started to leave the classroom," Tony mumbled, trying hard to concentrate. "Then I realized I didn't have any film, so I asked Mr. Cunningham—" He turned and faced left. "That's when Zach walked in." Tony looked back over his shoulder. "Mr. C tossed the film to—" Tony's eyes widened suddenly as he turned and pointed at Zach. "*You've* got the film!" he shouted. "Mr. C threw it to you!"

Kit giggled as Tony's face turned various shades of crimson. Zach was laughing so hard that he almost started to choke, and Kit had to pound him on the back.

"Okay, Mr. Zachary Taylor, ol' buddy," Tony snapped, snatching the box of film from Zach's outstretched hand. "That's it for you. No more Mr. Nice Guy." He narrowed his eyes. "As editor in chief of the *Spectator*, I'm assigning you both to interview Mr. Purvis."

The smiles were wiped instantly from Kit's and Zach's faces.

"Oh, no!" Kit pleaded. "You wouldn't!"

Tony stared unflinchingly at the two of them

for a long moment. Then a smug grin creased his face. "You're right, I wouldn't. But I just wanted you guys to recognize who you're dealing with!"

"Yes, sir!" Kit and Zach chorused, snapping off crisp salutes.

"That's better," Tony said. The automatic loader on the camera whirred as he slipped the film into its chamber. Then he gestured toward the door of the gym. "Shall we?"

Blue cushioned mats were spread out over most of the gym floor. At one end, the balance beam and vaulting horse were set up, and nearest the door stood the uneven parallel bars. The center area was reserved for the floor routines.

"There she is!" Kit pointed at her friend, who was poised on the edge of the large mat designated for the floor routine. Wearing a purple-and-pink leotard with matching pink tights, Jessica stood stock-still, focusing all of her concentration on the mat before her.

"We can watch her routine from here," Kit whispered to Tony and Zach. "Then we could go sit up in the bleachers for the rest of the workout."

Tony nodded and moved quietly across the floor to the edge of the mat, just as Jessica's music began.

Inhaling deeply Jessica raised up on her toes and then pounded diagonally across the mat into a round-off, back handspring, and dramatic double back flip.

"Look at her fly!" Kit said breathlessly, glancing at Zach over her shoulder.

Zach didn't reply. His eyes were glued on Jessica as she plunged into the splits. Then, turning gracefully, she raised herself into a full handstand.

The music slowed as Jessica moved into the adagio section of her program. Her cheeks flushed pink from exertion, she darted and danced to the romantic strains of a Chopin waltz, her every movement as precise and delicate as that of a ballerina.

The tempo changed again, and Kit felt proud as she watched her friend finish up her exercise with a brisk full back layout. Jessica landed softly on the mat with her arms outstretched and a glowing smile on her face.

There was a moment of silence before the gym echoed with applause. As Jessica's teammates rushed to hug her, she glanced up and spotted Kit and Zach on the sidelines. She waved to them, then draped a towel around her neck and stepped toward the far edge of the mat.

"That was awesome!" Zach shook his head.

The look of complete admiration in his eyes made Kit feel jealous. She turned away quickly. *Don't be silly,* she told herself. *How could Zach not be impressed?*

Jessica stepped lithely to the corner of the gym, where Ms. Ericksen was waiting to confer with her. The teacher gave her star athlete a hug, then gestured toward a tall, handsome boy dressed in a burgundy-and-gold warm-up suit who had been sitting in the first row of the bleachers throughout Jessica's routine.

"Who's that?" Kit asked, as Tony joined her and Zach up in the bleachers.

"That's Tuck Milligan," Tony answered, glancing in the direction Kit was indicating. "He's a freshman on the University of Washington gymnastics team. I think Coach Ericksen asked him here to watch Jessica."

"Milligan," Zach repeated thoughtfully. "Say, he's one of the guys everyone is predicting will be chosen for the next Olympic team."

"Are you positive about that?" Kit asked, her pen poised.

"Sure," Zach replied. "It's pretty hard to forget a nickname like Tuck."

Before Zach had even finished his sentence, Tony was scurrying across the floor to get a picture of Jessica in conversation with the star gymnast.

Kit and Zach laughed at Tony's eagerness and then sat down in the center of the bleachers. Kit dropped her bag on the wooden bench beside her, and a loud clunk reverberated through the room.

"What have you got in there?" Zach asked. "A bowling ball?"

"Nope!" Kit laughed. "Just a few important things."

"Let me guess," Zach said, reaching over to poke her book bag. "Makeup. A mirror, hairbrush—"

"Hey," Kit protested, "I'm a reporter, remember? Not a model."

"In that case—" Zach hefted the bag and said, "I've got it! A twenty-pound fountain pen and a lifetime supply of writing paper."

"Close." Kit flipped open the bag and allowed Zach to peer inside. A portable cassette recorder with two microphones took most of the space, but stuffed all around the recorder were yellow legal pads, several pencils and pens fastened together with a big thick rubber band, and a couple of back copies of the *Spectator*.

"My apologies for implying that you were frivolous," Zach said solemnly.

Kit tried to keep a straight face, but she burst into giggles as she unzipped another compartment to show Zach three brushes, a striped makeup bag, a little cracked hand mirror, and an old wrapper from a Snickers bar.

Zack laughed along with her, and they both turned their attention back to the mat where Tuck Milligan made Jessica go through her back layout again as he spotted her. This time she leapt higher than ever, and Kit gasped.

"Wow!" Zach said in awe. "That girl sure is something!"

"I hope Tony caught that picture," Kit said, scribbling furiously on her pad. "What do you think of 'Finch Flys High' as a potential headline?"

Zach paused to consider. "I like it!" he replied after a moment or two.

"Wait till you see Jess on the balance beam," Kit said. "You won't believe your eyes!"

"She must have a lot of self-discipline to be able to do all this," Zach mused as Jessica moved toward the vaulting horse.

"Jess is pretty serious about everything she does," Kit said. "But she's no stick-in-the-mud, either," she added quickly.

Zach nodded absently.

"But you know that," Kit continued, "from when you guys went out yesterday."

Zach cleared his throat. "I, uh, really didn't talk to her much." He glanced off to one side and muttered, "My mind went completely blank."

"Don't worry," Kit said, waving her hand airily. "You'll get to know her better on your next date."

"Date!" Zach repeated in a feeble croak.

"Maybe you guys could go for a soda again," Kit began, "only this time—"

"No way!" Zach interrupted. "You know that whole thing was a disaster!"

His vehemence made her blush. "Well, that's just because you hardly knew each other," Kit replied, recovering quickly. She'd ruined Jessica's first date, and she had to make it up to her by arranging a second one. "Maybe it was just too casual."

"Casual?" Zach repeated. "I never felt so formal in my whole life!"

"Well, how can anybody feel relaxed at a place filled with kids from school?"

"Boy, that's the truth!" Zach shook his head.

Kit pursed her lips thoughtfully. "What you need is someplace more romantic. You know, candlelight, soft music—"

"Whoa!" Zach cut in. "Now you're talking about a real date."

"Of course I am," Kit began, but seeing the anguished look on Zach's face she added quickly, "Relax. Thousands of kids go out on dates every Friday night—and live to tell about them."

"Gee," Zach said, "I wouldn't know what to do."

"What did you do in Portland?" Kit countered.

Zach shrugged. "I didn't date."

"What?" Kit blurted out, "A good-looking guy like you?"

Why had she said that? Kit watched as the tips of Zach's ears turned red.

"Well, a bunch of us did things together," Zach said, avoiding her eyes. "But they were never official dates. I don't think I'd know how to handle a real one, to tell you the truth."

"I'll help you," Kit heard herself saying.

Zach raised his eyebrows. "And how would you do that?"

"Well," Kit stammered, thinking fast, "we—we could go on a practice date, like we did with the soda shop."

"Yeah, you saw how well that turned out." Zach looked dubious.

"This will be really different," Kit insisted. "We can work out the entire evening in ad-

119

vance. You know, scout out the location and everything, just the way they do for the movies. Nothing will be left to chance, I swear. You couldn't go wrong!"

Zach took a deep breath. Kit met his gaze steadily, wondering how a boy could have such long eyelashes.

Finally he nodded. "Okay. Let's do it."

"That's great!" Kit felt tingly all over at the prospect of spending a day alone with Zach, even if it was just a practice date for him and Jessica.

"Meet me tomorrow at one o'clock at Pike Place Market," Kit said, hopping off the bench, "and we'll scout out restaurants and things together."

"That's it for today!" Ms. Ericksen's voice boomed out over the gym. "Good workout, everybody!"

With a start, Kit realized that she and Zach had completely missed the rest of Jessica's practice. For a second she couldn't even spot her friend down on the gym floor.

"Who are those guys?" Zach pointed toward the balance beam, where a thicket of boys were clustered. Jessica appeared to be the object of their attention.

"I don't believe it!" Kit muttered under her breath.

"Are they with the *Spectator*, too?" Zach asked.

Kit nodded as she watched Jerry Gill and two other boys from the staff jostling around Jessica. Each of them had a camera and note pad, and they were all frantically snapping pictures of her and shouting questions over the hubbub.

"This assignment has been taken!" Tony's voice carried across the gym. "Who's the editor here, anyway?"

Kit shook her head. "They all must have gotten wind that Mr. Purvis was going to talk to them."

Tony kept bobbing up from the clump of bodies, his face red with anger. Jerry and the other boys were gesturing wildly and pointing to their cameras.

"Those jerks!" Kit grinned at Zach. "They must have figured that Mr. Purvis couldn't accuse them of slacking off if they showed up with material at the meeting on Monday.

"I don't think anybody's going to get too many pictures." Zach pointed to Jessica, who was standing off in the corner, a towel draped around her neck, laughing easily with Tuck Milligan. The two of them slipped out of the gym together and into Coach Ericksen's office. Tony and his reporters were apparently so busy arguing that they never even noticed.

"I guess we should go, too," Zach said, easing his lanky frame off the hardwood bleacher. Kit gathered up her gear, and they pushed their way through the gym and out into the hall.

"So, where shall we meet?" Zach asked.

Kit looked up at him uncomprehendingly.

Zach frowned. "At the market. Where exactly should we meet? It's a big place, you know."

"Oh!" Kit thought for a moment. "At the big flower stall, I guess. You can't miss it."

Zach nodded. "One o'clock, then." To Kit's surprise he winked. "Be there!"

Chapter Twelve

"Why do these things always happen to me?" Kit wailed as her bus lurched to a halt in the heavy downtown traffic. It was already quarter past one, and the Pike Place Market was a good ten-minute walk away. "Hurry up, hurry up!" she begged between clenched teeth.

The bus responded with a sudden leap forward, followed by a squeal of brakes and angry honking of car horns. Impulsively, Kit yanked the bell cord, and the driver opened the rear exit. Jumping down to the pavement, she edged around a stalled taxicab and hurried off down Third Avenue.

Saturday morning had not gone well. First of all, Kit hadn't been able to find a thing to wear. She'd wanted to look nice, but she didn't want Zach to think she had dressed up especially for him. On the other hand, she didn't want to look frumpy, either. Kit had finally decided on baggy pink jeans with red suspenders, a white cotton blouse, and her long pink coat.

At least the weather was cooperating. The sun shone brightly through the crisp air, and Kit's spirits began to lift as she neared the market. Turning the corner at Pike Street, she headed west toward the Sound. The familiar old brick buildings of the market came into view, and Kit picked up her pace.

Pike Place Market rested at the top of a low hill above the waterfront where Kit, Zach, Tony, and Jessica had been the week before. The market was a maze of shops and stalls that sold fresh fish, crab, salmon, and mussels along with fresh fruit and vegetables. There were plenty of specialty shops as well, and at least a dozen flower stalls.

Finally Kit spied Zach's blond head bobbing through the milling crowd. An old Chinese man was strolling beside him, pushing a cart filled with freshly cut flowers.

"Zach!" Kit shouted, waving to catch his eye. "Zachery Taylor!"

Zach turned, startled, at the sound of his name. His face broke into a grin as he spotted Kit, and he motioned for her to join him.

Kit dove into the bustling crowd, and moments later she found herself beside Zach and the old Chinese man.

"Boy, I was afraid I wouldn't find you!" Kit gasped, bending over a bit to catch her breath. "I'd forgotten how many flower stalls there are in this place."

"Tell me about it." Zach chuckled and gestured to the tiny man beside him. "I finally attached myself to Mr. Lo, here. I figured I'd spot you better strolling through the market than just waiting around in some corner."

Mr. Lo smiled at Kit and bowed deeply. "Ah! Is this the beautiful girl you were telling me about, Zach?"

Zach blushed and mumbled something incomprehensible. Kit jumped in quickly to spare him any more embarrassment. "No, no! I'm the beautiful girl's best friend."

"Kit Carson, meet Benjamin Lo," Zach said, recovering quickly.

"Pleased to meet you, Mr. Lo," Kit shook his hand.

"Please, call me Ben." The flower seller pulled a bright red carnation from his cart and presented it to Kit with a flourish. "If you, who are so lovely, are the beautiful girl's best friend, I cannot imagine what she must look like."

"Take my word for it, she's a knockout,"

Kit said matter-of-factly. She inhaled the wonderful scent of the carnation before tucking the bloom behind her ear.

Kit turned to Zach. "Well, I guess we should get right down to business."

"How can we scout places out on an empty stomach?" Zach said, clutching his middle in mock agony.

"Well, if you're so hungry, go get something to eat." Kit gestured vaguely toward the food stands.

"All alone?" Zach grimaced and turned back to Mr. Lo. "What do you suggest I do about this, Ben?"

"Perhaps another flower?" Ben pulled a long-stemmed pink carnation from a pail and gave it to Zach. "One for each ear."

Zach handed the flower to Kit, who stared at it dumbly. Zach was acting so strangely that she wasn't sure how to respond.

Zach motioned to Kit. "Stay put. I'll be right back."

Still clutching her carnation, Kit watched as Zach made his way over to a French bakery and bought a long loaf of bread. Then he lined up at the deli counter next door and ordered three different types of cheese. A couple of bottles of soda and a pint of Alaskan strawberries came next. Kit looked over at Ben in amazement. He just winked.

Soon Zach was back, his arms full of paper bags.

"Will you have lunch with me?"

Kit decided to play along with Zach's little game. "Sure," she agreed. "But I get to pick the place."

"Fair enough."

The two of them said good-bye to Mr. Lo, and Kit led Zach through the crush of Saturday shoppers and tourists.

"Where are you taking us?" Zach asked, scrambling to keep up with her.

"I've got something in mind!" Kit replied. "Trust me!"

Without waiting for his answer, she ran toward the market's waterfront level. Soon they were walking down Alaskan Way, heading south along the edge of Elliott Bay.

"Hey, we've already been down here," Zach said as they passed the familiar storefront of Ye Olde Curiousity Shoppe. "I thought we were supposed to be scouting new locations."

Kit held her index finger to her lips with a warning look, and Zach mimed a zipper being fastened across his mouth. Soon they were crossing a large parking lot.

"There!" Kit pointed triumphantly toward the water. "There's the cheapest ticket to adventure and romance in Seattle!"

As if on cue, a blast from a ship's horn greeted them. Zach turned to watch as a giant Puget Sound ferry glided toward its landing slip.

"We can take the ferry over to Winslow on Bainbridge Island," Kit explained excitedly. "It only takes fifteen minutes." Suddenly remembering the real reason for their outing, she added quickly, "Once we're there we'll find a really romantic restaurant for you and Jessica."

"Let's go!" Zach replied, striding up the escalator that led to the ticket station and the passenger-loading area.

A few minutes later Kit and Zach stood on the observation deck, the brisk ocean breeze nearly blowing them away. As the ferry moved out of Elliott Bay into the more open waters of Puget Sound, it began to roll gently from side to side. To their left Kit and Zach could see the old-fashioned lighthouse off Alki Point, with its spotless white walls and red roof.

"Hey, look at that mountain!" Zach shouted, pointing to the southwest.

Kit grinned. He had to be talking about Mt. Rainier, the tallest peak in the Northwest. Since the mountain was often obscured by clouds, it was a real treat to see its snow-capped rim. The extinct volcano loomed in the southern sky, looking almost like an ice-cream cone.

"The Indians believed that their gods lived along its slopes," Kit said.

Zach nodded, impressed by the panorama before him. "I don't blame them." Then he looked at Kit and smiled. "The gods must be smiling on our expedition. We should feel honored."

Before Kit could reply, they were interrupted by a raucous squawk from off the port bow. A flock of gulls was soaring in the strong wind, hovering above the waves before dipping into the spray and coming up again with tiny fish.

"Watch this!" Zach reached into one of the bags and tore off the heel from the loaf of bread. He leaned over the railing and held out the crust toward the gulls. Immediately one of them peeled away from the others and soared toward Zach's outstretched hand. The bird hovered for a moment above Zach's hand, then dipped down and snatched the bread.

Zach whooped loudly as the bird, pursued by two others, dipped away with its prize. There was a brief aerial dogfight, which culminated in a crash into the waves. Kit and Zach laughed as the surprised gulls ruffled their feathers.

After Kit and Zach disembarked at Winslow, they headed down the street that bordered the island's little bay.

"There are some great restaurants along here," Kit said, trying to remain businesslike. "We shouldn't have any trouble picking the perfect one for you and Jessica."

"Wait a minute!" Zach protested. "I am not going to carry these provisions all over the island." They were standing on a wooden walkway which led from the ferry dock to dry land. He held the bags over the railing. "Either we eat now, or this stuff goes into the drink!"

Kit laughed and held up her hands in mock defeat. "Okay, okay, you win!"

They walked down to the water's edge and sat down on a green, grassy bank. Soon they were devouring the cheese and bread with a vengeance.

"Do you ever wonder what your parents were like when they were in high school?" asked Kit suddenly.

"I've seen pictures of my dad in his yearbook." Zach chuckled. "He was tall and a lot skinnier than he is now. Kind of goofy looking. He's an English professor now—always quoting Byron, Shelley, or Keats. People say we look a whole lot alike," Zach added mournfully.

"You're not goofy looking!" Kit protested. "Tall and thin yes. But definitely not goofy looking."

"Thank you." Zach tipped an invisible hat and grinned smugly.

"That doesn't mean you can go and get a swelled head about it," Kit shot back.

Zach rolled his eyes. "I won't. That's a promise!"

Kit laughed before confiding, "My dad was president of the nerd society. You know, he was one of those guys who carry a briefcase, wear pen holders, and have a million mechanical pencils in their shirt pockets." She shook her head. "He's a design engineer now— always scribbling figures on envelopes and magazine covers. But he certainly marched to a different drummer."

"Kind of like his daughter," Zach said quietly.

"What do you mean?" Kit demanded, tossing a handful of grass at him. "Do I act like a nerd?"

"Of course not!" He shook his head emphatically. "But you *are* different, you know."

Kit frowned. "Gramps said something like that the other day. Different, in a good way or bad?" she asked cautiously, holding her breath.

"Definitely good!" he replied. Before Kit could reply he added, grinning wickedly, "But don't get a swelled head about it!"

The two of them stretched out on their stomachs and stared at the rippling waters of the Sound, sharing a comfortable silence.

"This was a great idea, Kit," Zach said after a while. "I can't remember when I've had such a good time doing nothing."

"I know what you mean," Kit murmured lazily, wishing the moment would last forever. Then she jerked upright. "Wait a minute! What are we doing? We've got work to do!" She leapt up and brushed the twigs off her pants. "Come on!"

For the rest of the afternoon they prowled up and down the quaint streets of the little town, comparing menus in the windows of different restaurants and poking around inside the shops, planning each segment of the proposed date with Jessica.

Kit noticed that, while she did all the work, Zach was content to ramble along beside her, agreeing with each suggestion she made.

"It's almost six o'clock," Kit said finally, examining her watch. "By this time you and Jess would have finished dinner, and you'd be strolling back along the street to catch the ferry."

"Okay." Zach nodded amiably. Then, to Kit's surprise, he offered her his arm. She hesitated.

"It seems like the appropriate thing to do, don't you think?" he asked, interpreting her reluctance as a refusal. "Or am I being silly?"

"No, no," Kit said hastily. At least he was finally getting into the spirit of the excursion. "That's a great idea. Any girl would love that. It's very romantic and chivalrous."

"I'll make a note of that," Zach replied.

A blast from the ship's horn reminded them to hurry back to the ferry slip, and the moment's awkwardness evaporated in their rush to board. As if by unspoken agreement, Kit and Zach walked directly to the place in the bow where they had ridden before.

Daylight was fading fast. The glass towers of the city glowed like molten gold in the setting sun. Tiny lights flickered along the shoreline, and the blue of the sky was now as deep as the blue of the bay. Kit and Zach stood together along the rail, awed to silence by the beauty.

"You know," Zach said slowly, "if there was ever a moment when a guy should kiss a girl"—he cleared his throat huskily, then continued—"this is it."

Kit's heart fluttered wildly, hoping that he meant her. She could feel Zach's warm presence next to her, so close and yet so far away. The cool wind whipped her hair around her face, and the crispness of the air made her eyes water. Their hands gripped the rail side by side, almost touching. Kit forced herself to look straight ahead and stare reality in the face.

She was in love with Zach. Totally, uncontrollably, irrevocably in love. And there was nothing she could do about it. In a few days Zach would go out with Jessica, and the perfect match she had made would be complete. They'd meet at the market—perhaps he'd buy her a flower, too, then take her across to Bainbridge Island, just as Kit had planned for them to do. And, on the way back, he'd take her in his arms and . . .

Kit shuddered violently. Zach, startled at the movement, asked, "Is anything wrong? Are you cold?"

"I guess I am a little cold," she replied, feeling more alone than ever. "Let's go inside, okay?"

Zach nodded but didn't say anything. He held open the door leading into the main cabin, and they sat down at one of the tables in the lounge. They passed the remaining minutes of the trip quietly, wrapped in their own thoughts.

They stepped off the ferry and made their way up to the bus stop.

"Zach, listen," Kit began. He turned to look at her expectantly, and her voice failed. She felt as if they were saying good-bye forever. "Thanks for lunch," she said, "and the carnations—"

Kit reached up and took one of the flowers from her hair and very carefully tucked it into the buttonhole of Zach's jacket.

"There!" she murmured, patting his lapel. "Now we each have a souvenir."

The squeal of brakes behind her made Kit turn to see her bus pull up to the curb.

"See you Monday!" Kit called as she hopped on, the doors sliding shut behind her. She hurried all the way to the back so she could wave as the bus pulled away.

Zach stood alone on the pavement. When she waved, he raised a hand in a farewell salute.

Chapter Thirteen

Meet me at my locker before lunch. Big news!

—Jessica

With a heavy heart, Kit reread the note she'd found taped to her locker that morning, then tucked it away in her book bag. She could guess what the big news was. Zach must have asked Jessica out. The practice date had been a success, but she felt miserable.

Jessica was already waiting when Kit arrived. Her eyes were shining with suppressed excitement.

"Kit," she began, her voice sounding slightly breathless, "I'm in love!"

"I'm not surprised," Kit replied, trying to

smile at her friend's happiness. "He's a great guy."

"Don't you think he's terrific?" Jessica said dreamily, hugging her books to her chest.

"Oh, sure!" Kit answered. *More than you'll ever know,* she added silently.

"I mean, I never thought I could feel this way," Jessica gushed.

"Oh, I knew right away that you two would hit it off," Kit said. "So did everyone else."

"You know, he really *is* different from all the other guys," Jessica continued, spinning the combination on her locker and opening the door. Kit could see shelves covered with workout clothes, rolls of athletic tape, and worn dance shoes. "He's funny and thoughtful, and strong and sensitive."

Kit nodded, blinking back tears. It was true. Zach was all those things and more. And now she could never have him.

"We spent all day Sunday together," Jessica was saying. "And we had a fabulous time!"

"Sunday?" Kit repeated in astonishment. Zach must have called Jessica Saturday night, right after he'd gotten home from their practice date at the market.

"He even gave me Mortimer Monkey for luck at the tournament!" Jessica pulled a small stuffed monkey with a plaid ribbon bow around its neck out of her locker.

"Wow," Kit said, swallowing hard. "He sure moves fast!"

Jessica giggled. "I know it seems kind of sudden," she said, "but we just clicked the minute we saw each other." She gave the stuffed animal a squeeze. "I don't think it's any big deal that he's two years older, do you?"

"Two years older?" Kit fell back against the bank of blue metal lockers.

"I know it seems like a lot," Jessica continued, "but when I'm with him, I don't feel the age difference at all!"

Kit's brain was reeling. How could Zach be nineteen? He must have been held back in school for some reason.

"What's the matter, Kit?" Jessica asked, sounding concerned.

"It's—it's just so hard to believe he's two years older than we are," Kit stammered. "I mean, he seems pretty well adjusted."

Jessica frowned. "Why wouldn't he be?"

"Well, if he got held back in school and all—" Kit's voice trailed off.

"He didn't get held back," Jessica said, looking a little annoyed. "If anything, he's an overachiever. I mean, he's on the dean's list at UW and—"

"He goes to high school *and* college?" Kit was astonished.

"Kit Carson!" Jessica said impatiently, "What are you talking about?"

But Kit wasn't listening. She paced up and down the corridor, muttering, "He never said anything about that! Boy, you think you know somebody, and then you find out something like this. I mean, he told me he'd never even dated before!"

"Kit, will you be quiet for one second?" Jessica shouted suddenly.

Kit jerked up her head and stared at her friend.

"I don't think we're talking about the same person," Jessica said slowly.

"Of course we are," Kit insisted. "Zachary Taylor. I just had no idea that he was older, and going to college—"

"He's not," Jessica interrupted. "Tuck is."

"Tuck?" Kit repeated, uncomprehending. "Who's he?"

"The person I've been trying to tell you about for the past ten minutes," Jessica said. "The guy I'm in love with, for heaven's sake."

"Oh, no!" The realization hit Kit like a sledge hammer. "You're involved with *Tuck Milligan*?"

Jessica nodded.

"But what about Zach?" Kit demanded.

Jessica looked confused. "What about him?"

"How could you do this to him?"

"What do you mean? I haven't done anything."

"*Haven't done anything!*" Kit sputtered with indignation. "You told me yourself that you wanted to go out with the guy."

"That was before I met Tuck."

"Boy," Kit fumed, "you really are Miss Fickle Finch! I mean you just drop him like a hot potato—"

"Wait a minute, Kit!" Jessica cut in calmly. "Zach and I went out for a soda together once, and it was disastrous. We bored each other to death."

"How can you call Zach boring?" Kit asked.

"I didn't say *he* was boring!" Jessica replied. "He seems like a lot of fun when he's with you."

"Well, that's because we're friends."

"Gosh, Kit." Jessica shook her head in frustration. "There's no reason for *you* to be so upset. You act as if you're in love with him or something."

"I am not!" Kit protested a little too loudly. "And anyway, it doesn't matter how *I* feel!"

Kit's words seemed caught in her throat as she fought hard to keep the tears from over-whelming her. "Zach likes *you*. And he'll be heartbroken when he finds out about you and Tuck!"

"I really don't think Zach will care," Jessica said, looking at the ceiling.

"That shows how much *you* know!" Kit realized her nose was starting to run, and she groped in her purse for a tissue. "We went on a practice date together and every-thing, just to make sure you two would have the perfect evening."

"You did *what*?"

Kit realized she sounded ridiculous. "Lis-ten, I'd better go," she said, backing away. "The bell's going to ring."

"I don't understand why you're so angry," Jessica said, her own eyes growing misty.

"I'm not mad, Jessica," Kit managed to say. "It's just that . . ." Her voice trailed off.

How could she explain how she felt? She'd been an idiot for leading Zach on, making him believe that Jessica liked him. "Now he'll probably hate me!" Kit started to sob.

Suddenly the bell rang, and students be-gan to fill the hall. Kit lowered her head and moved quickly in the direction of her next class.

"Kit, please wait!" she heard Jessica call, but she kept on hurrying down the corridor until her friend's voice was lost in the noise of the crowd.

The journalism room was deathly quiet when Kit stepped through the door. Tony and Mel were already hard at work, and the only sound was the tap-tapping of typewriters. The skin on the back of Kit's neck prickled from the tension in the air.

"How'd you guys get here so soon?" she asked, dropping her bag on her desk.

"I've been here all day," Tony mumbled, not looking up from his typewriter.

"So have I," Mel snapped, laboring over the pasteup of the advertising section. "Ever since the disaster."

"Disaster?" Kit repeated, slipping on her white lab coat. "What are you talking about?"

"Just ask the Hardy Boys," Tony grumbled, jerking his thumb over his shoulder. "They got this bright idea at the computer fair to simplify our system—only they jammed it. Everything's in there, but we can't get at it."

Kit glanced toward the computer station, where Brian and Sam sat, jaws clenched, watching Mr. Cunningham pound away at the terminal. The full weight of Tony's statement finally hit her.

"Everything?" she whispered. "You mean that two weeks of work is gone!"

"You got it," Zach said.

He was standing by the door, looking drawn and serious. At the sound of his voice, Kit remembered her conversation with Jessica, and her stomach knotted into a tight ball.

"Why is it I'm always the last to know about everything?" Kit demanded.

"We tried to find you at lunch," Melanie explained, "but you weren't in the cafeteria."

"Need I remind everyone that time is ticking away?" Tony interrupted, his face pinched and haggard looking. "Do something!"

Kit looked about helplessly. "Where do we begin?"

"You concentrate on rewriting 'Kit's Korner,' " Tony ordered. "And, Zach, you'd better tackle the Jessica Project by yourself."

It's already beginning to happen, Kit thought to herself. *We're not working together anymore.*

Kit pulled the cover off of the old Underwood typewriter on her desk and quickly rolled a blank sheet of paper into the carriage.

"The only thing we have to work with are the photos," Tony said, ducking into the darkroom and reappearing with a stack of pictures. "Unfortunately, they're all of Jessica."

"How'd that happen?" Melanie asked. "You'd think she was the only student at Queen Anne High."

"Jerry Gill got a bright idea that, if he photographed Jessica, Mr. Purvis would think he was an active member of the paper," Kit explained.

"Which he isn't," Tony barked. "He can't even take a decent photo. Look at this one!" He held up a blurry shot. "This one—it's Jerry's thumb."

"I'm sure Jerry also thought it would give him a chance to get close to Jessica," Kit added. "Which it didn't. She turned him down—"

"Hey, I thought you and Jerry were pretty close," Zach interrupted.

"Jerry?" Kit asked. "Whatever gave you that idea?"

"Well, the first day I was here, you had to go talk to him—"

"Oh, *that!*" Kit dismissed the event with a wave of her hand. "He wanted to talk to me about Jessica. Just like every other boy in this school."

"Really?" Zach's face lit up suddenly, and Kit went white.

Oh, no, she thought, *I've still got to break it to him about Jessica. He'll never forgive me.*

Zach's voice cut through her thoughts, demanding, "So, what about Burke?"

"Burke Walker?" Kit asked, totally taken aback.

Zach nodded vigorously.

"What about him?" she stammered.

"Are you two dating?" Zach was grilling her like a hard-core reporter.

A loud snort came from Tony, who was back at his typewriter but listening in on their conversation.

"That noise from Tony translates into 'Burke has been going steady with Rhonda White for the past two years.' I introduced them."

"Wait a minute!" Zach broke in, his voice low and urgent. "Does that mean that you're not seeing anyone?"

"No, of course I'm not!" Kit suddenly felt embarrassed. Was he trying to humiliate her in front of everybody? "What is this, Twenty Questions?"

"It sure sounds like it," Melanie remarked from the pasteup table.

"How does anyone have a private conversation around here?" Zach demanded, opening his arms wide and turning to face the staff.

Without looking at him, the entire group pointed to the door at the far end of the room marked Dark Room.

Zach grabbed Kit by the hand, led her through the door, and shut it firmly behind him.

The room was lit by a single red bulb, giving Kit an eerie feeling.

"Now," Zach said, "you and I have to talk! What is going on?" He crossed his arms and looked Kit straight in the eye.

Kit felt her stomach sink like a stone. *This is the end*, she thought. *He knows about Tuck and Jessica!*

"If it's about Jessica," Kit said, her lip starting to quiver dangerously, "I'm really sorry. I had no idea!"

"What?" Zach ran his hand through his hair and took a deep breath.

"I had no idea, really." Kit backed up against the sink. "I just wanted things to work out—"

"What are you talking about?" Zach exclaimed, looking more agitated than ever.

"Jessica and Tuck are seeing each other," Kit burst out, gesturing at the newly developed pictures of them, hanging up to dry around the darkroom. Tony's camera had caught the couple laughing as they worked

147

together. It was painfully obvious how crazy they were about each other.

"I wanted you guys to get together so much," Kit babbled on nervously, "I guess I was blind—"

"Wait a minute!" Zach held his hand up. "Why did you want Jessica and me to get together?"

Kit took a deep breath. "Because Jessica said she liked you. You saw her picture and went nuts over it and . . ." Kit's voice trailed off.

Zach was shaking his head, a huge grin on his face.

"What are you laughing at?" Kit demanded, putting her hands on her hips. Why was he making fun of her?

Zach chuckled. "You and your dumb match-making scheme!" He crossed his arms and leaned against the wall, staring at her.

"If it was so dumb," Kit shot back defensively, "then why did *you* go along with it?"

"Because"—Zach took a deep breath and stared down at his shoes—"because . . ." He started again, beginning to pace the tiny room. "I mean, if you really want to know—"

"Yes, I do," Kit said. She wanted to hear the whole truth, no matter how bad it was.

Zach faced Kit and shrugged helplessly. "I've

only been going along with this practice-date stuff to be near you," he mumbled.

The room seemed to be spinning. Kit grabbed hold of the edge of the sink to steady herself. Was her mind playing tricks on her? "What did you say?" she asked, barely whispering.

Zach took a step toward her. "I'm crazy about you."

"What?" Kit gasped.

"Aw, come on, don't make me say it again!" Zach protested. "That was pure agony!"

Kit felt her eyes brimming with tears.

"I've been crazy about you from the moment I saw you," Zach said softly, taking her hand. "But I figured you were already involved with someone. Then, when you wanted me to date Jessica, I was sure of it."

"Oh, Zach," Kit murmured, not daring to move. They were standing so close together that she was sure he could hear her heart beating.

"Remember on the boat," Zach whispered huskily, "I said if there was ever a moment when a guy should kiss a girl, that that was it?"

Kit nodded, unable to tear her eyes from his face.

"Well, I was wrong." Slowly Zach leaned forward and, just before his lips met hers, he murmured, "This is."

His kiss was soft and gentle, and Kit allowed him to fold her in his arms, losing all sense of time and place.

Suddenly a cheer erupted from the classroom, followed by a loud pounding on the darkroom door.

"Mr. C's got the computer up!" Tony yelled. "Let's go, you two. We've got a paper to get out! What are you *doing* in there, anyway?"

Kit looked into Zach's eyes, and their lips met again. The newsroom suddenly seemed very far away. *We're falling in love,* she answered silently. *And we may stay here forever.*

EXCITING NEWS FOR ROMANCE READERS

Loveletters—the all new, hot-off-the-press Romance Newsletter. Now you can be the first to know:

What's Coming Up:
* Exciting offers
* New romance series on the way

What's Going Down:
* The latest gossip about the SWEET VALLEY HIGH gang
* Who's in love . . . and who's not
* What Loveletters fans are saying.

Who's New:
* Be on the inside track for upcoming titles

If you don't already receive Loveletters, fill out this coupon, mail it in, and you will receive Loveletters several times a year. Loveletters . . . you're going to love it!

Please send me my free copy of Loveletters

Name _____ Date of Birth _____

Address _____

City _____ State _____ Zip _____

To: LOVELETTERS
BANTAM BOOKS
PO BOX 1005
SOUTH HOLLAND, IL 60473

SWEET DREAMS are fresh, fun and exciting—alive with the flavor of the contemporary teen scene—the joy and doubt of *first love*. If you've missed any SWEET DREAMS titles, then you're missing out on *your* kind of stories, written about people like *you!*

☐ 26293	HEART TO HEART #118 Stefanie Curtis		$2.50
☐ 26339	STAR-CROSSED LOVE #119 Sharon Cadwallader		$2.50
☐ 26340	MR. WONDERFUL #120 Fran Michaels		$2.50
☐ 26418	ONLY MAKE-BELIEVE #121 Julia Winfield		$2.50
☐ 26419	STARS IN HER EYES #122 Dee Daley		$2.50
☐ 26481	LOVE IN THE WINGS #123 Virginia Smiley		$2.50
☐ 26482	MORE THAN FRIENDS #124 Janice Boies		$2.50
☐ 26528	PARADE OF HEARTS #125 Cloverdale Press		$2.50
☐ 26566	HERE'S MY HEART #126 Stefanie Curtis		$2.50
☐ 26567	MY BEST ENEMY #127 Janet Quin-Harkin		$2.50
☐ 26671	ONE BOY AT A TIME #128 Diana Gregory		$2.50
☐ 26672	A VOTE FOR LOVE #129 Terri Fields		$2.50
☐ 26701	DANCE WITH ME #130 Jahnna Beecham		$2.50
☐ 26865	HAND-ME-DOWN HEART #131 Mary Schultz		$2.50
☐ 26790	WINNER TAKES ALL #132 Laurie Lykken		$2.50
☐ 26864	PLAYING THE FIELD #133 Eileen Hehl		$2.50
☐ 26789	PAST PERFECT #134 Fran Michaels		$2.50
☐ 26902	GEARED FOR ROMANCE #135 Shan Finney		$2.50
☐ 26903	STAND BY FOR LOVE #136	Carol MacBain	$2.50
☐ 26948	ROCKY ROMANCE #137 Sharon Dennis Wyeth		$2.50
☐ 26949	HEART & SOUL #138	Janice Boies	$2.50
☐ 27005	THE RIGHT COMBINATION #139 Jahnna Beecham		$2.50
☐ 27061	LOVE DETOUR #140	Stefanie Curtis	$2.50
☐ 27062	WINTER DREAMS #141	Barbara Conklin	$2.50

Prices and availability subject to change without notice.

- - - - - - - - - - - - - - - -

Bantam Books, Dept. SD, 414 East Golf Road, Des Plaines, IL 60016

Please send me the books I have checked above. I am enclosing $_____
(please add $2.00 to cover postage and handling). Send check or money order
—no cash or C.O.D.s please.

Mr/Ms _____

Address_____

City/State _____ Zip _____

SD—5/88

Please allow four to six weeks for delivery. This offer expires 11/88.